ISLE ROYALE CALLING

Helen H. Cloutier

ISLE ROYALE
CALLING

vvvv • vvvv • vvvv • vvvv • vvvv • vvvv • vvvv

WILLIAM B. EERDMANS PUBLISHING COMPANY
GRAND RAPIDS, MICHIGAN

© 1957 by Helen H. Cloutier
All rights reserved

The characters and situations in this book are wholly
fictional and imaginative; they do not portray and are
not intended to portray any actual persons or parties

First published by Dodd, Mead & Company, 1957
Reprinted by Wm. B. Eerdmans Publishing Company, 1966

Library of Congress Catalog Card Number: 57-11346

Printed in the United States of America

TO

Mom and Dad, John D., John H.,
and Charles H., and with love —

ACKNOWLEDGMENTS

My thanks, first of all, must go to Dorothy Bryan, my editor. But for her faith in me and my story, this book would still be gathering dust.

Then to my coaches, Louise B. Clancy of Detroit, who instilled the original idea during a casual conversation about her vacation on Isle Royale; to my ex-boss, Bill Duchaine, editor of the *Escanaba Daily Press* for twenty-five years, who gave me his own publicity files on Isle Royale; to the Department of the Interior for their co-operation in giving me information and the map; to the Coast Guard men who checked maps with me, discussed the probabilities and improbabilities of what could or couldn't happen to a ship, and for their stories of actual ships in distress; to my family, who listened to the clatter of the typewriter from nine o'clock every evening into the wee hours; to Professor Litten of Northwestern University, who coached, scolded and encouraged and who will never read this book; and to Governor G. Mennen Williams, who had the background thoroughly checked for authenticity before he endorsed this book on one of his favorite projects.

God Bless.

H. H. C.

FOREWORD

With a background begging to be explored, Isle Royale, the largest island in fresh water in the world, makes a perfect setting for a story of adventure.

Research for this book extended over fifteen years, ten complete rewrites—and many hours of sorting and discarding. A wealth of material, exciting and mysterious, was uncovered, some of which will be used in forthcoming books and stories.

Isle Royale, the only National Park located in Michigan, has a background extending back to a definite point in history. Beyond that, into the past, the history is completely unknown. Expeditions to the island have found traces of the Aztec tribes but no connecting link has been discovered. Did the Aztecs really migrate to the island? If so, when? And why is there no historical information on it? These questions and many more have given the island a history yet to be uncovered.

This story takes place on Isle Royale before it became a National Park, about the time when I was talking daily —via ham radio—to the Johnson girls who lived on the island. I have also talked—via ham radio—with the men who actually trapped the moose and who laughingly supplied information on how it was done.

The island is properly named, for it is, indeed, the Royal Island of the Great Lakes.

HELEN H. CLOUTIER

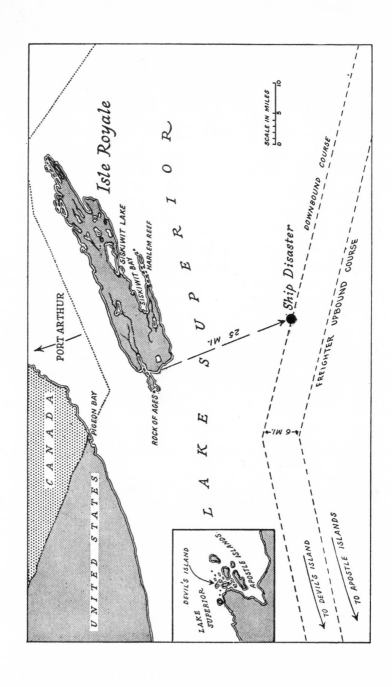

1

wwv • wwv • wwv • wwv • wwv • wwv • wwv

"But, Tom," Jim St. Cyr objected into
the microphone, "Dad doesn't want me to leave Isle Royale. He'll never let me go to school next summer at
Houghton!" The autumn sun caught the red fire of Jim's
hair and made it glisten like copper as he flipped the
transmitter switch. Despair gave his voice a low pitch.

The answer came eerily through the loudspeaker of
Jim's Hallicrafter amateur radio receiver. "For the love
of mike, how can he expect you to be a Forest Ranger like
he is—if you don't like it?" The voice paused. Jim ran his
fingers through his rumpled hair. Then the voice of his
friend on the mainland broke through the static again.
"I thought fathers were educated now . . . at least to the
point where they let their kids make up their own minds
about what they want to be! After all, you're seventeen.
You should know what you want to do!" The voice had a
sarcastic note in it.

Jim flipped the switch again. "W9XXM, this is W9ZZO.

You just don't understand, Tom. Dad has always had his heart set on one of us being a Ranger here on Isle Royale. After all—it's a pretty nice setup, and Mother wanted us to be together always." Jim's brusqueness vanished. His mother had died when his youngest brother, Charles, was a baby.

"Let him make a Ranger out of your kid brother, Chum. Anyone who's as handy with radio as you are has no business being sidetracked." The voice hesitated for an instant. "Well, I've got to sign off now, Jim. See you tomorrow. S'long. W9ZZO, this is W9XXM, over—off and clear."

"73, Tom. See you tomorrow. W9ZZO, Isle Royale, clear." Jim turned off the transmit switch to standby. He watched the light fade from the 814 tube in the final of the transmitter. He felt glassed in, like the light in the tube.

Jim had built his own radio shack the first summer he had had his radio license and since then—for almost three years—he had spent all his spare time talking to other amateur radio operators throughout the world.

The interior of the ham shack was a colorful hodge-podge. Postcards with huge, gaudy letters, papered the walls. Cards from every corner of the globe—from every state in the United States were carefully thumbtacked to the wallboard. There were G cards from England, F cards from France, GM cards from Scotland, LU cards from Luxemburg, cards from sixty-two different countries and each had its own place of honor.

The workbench along one wall was cluttered with spare radio parts, bits of wire, a soldering iron, tubes and a stack of battered and well-worn QST magazines.

Jim looked around. Pride of ownership made his eyes sparkle. This world of Ham Radio held a promise for him, adventure, excitement, contact with every part of the globe, every part of the country outside the island orbit.

He sighed softly. "Wonder how DX (distance) is today," he murmured as he turned the Hallicrafter SX 25 receiver to the 20 meter band and retuned the transmitter.

Yesterday DX on twenty meters had been terrific. He'd worked George in England and had held the QSO for over an hour. Next he'd talked with a W4/Marine Mobile off the coast of southern California, on the *S. S. Georgiana*, a freighter en route with a cargo for northern ports. Then a K7 in Alaska had called him with a message to relay to Detroit, Michigan. The list of entries on the open log covered half a page.

Signals boomed through as Jim slowly turned the vernier dials on the receiver. He bent over his desk, listening intently.

"Calling CQ, calling CQ, calling CQ twenty meters. CQ, CQ, CQ. This is W4AFV in Tampa, Florida, calling CQ and standing by. Come in someone, please."

Jim's fingers automatically reached for the plate switch on the transmitter and flipped it on. He glanced at the plate meter to see whether the antenna was loading properly.

"W4AFV, W4AFV, W4AFV. Calling W4AFV. This is W9ZZO, Isle Royale, calling W4AFV in Tampa. What say, old man? W9ZZO standing by."

He flipped the transmitter plate switch off and a relay switched the receiver on again.

"W9ZZO, this is W4AFV, Tampa, Florida, returning. Thanks very much for your call, old man. You're QSA 5 plus 20 DB here in Florida. Brother! What a signal. Sure pounding in down here. We've got some nice weather down here today, too—only about ninety-nine degrees. Sure wish I had some of that cool Superior breeze down here right now. The handle here is Hal. How's everything up there in W9 land? Don't believe we've ever QSO'd before, at least I can't seem to find your card in my file. How about it, old man? What's the QTH? W9ZZO, this is W4AFV standing by."

As Jim turned on the plate switch a smile curved the corners of his mouth. It was obvious that his heart was wrapped up in Ham radio.

"W4AFV, this is W9ZZO, Isle Royale—in Lake Superior, returning. Okay, Hal, very fine business. You sure are putting a fine signal up in Isle Royale today. I've heard you on several times before but I don't think I've ever talked with you. The rig here is a home-brewed job, running about 75 watts into a two element rotary beam— a plumber's delight, Hal. But have had pretty good luck with it so far. Got some nice DX on it, so guess it's perking pretty well. We're located on Isle Royale, out in Lake Superior. Dad's a Forest Ranger here and my brothers and I live and go to school on the island. Gets kinda lonesome, but ham radio fixes that up in a hurry. I'll be glad to swap cards with you, Hal. Just send it care of General Delivery, Copper Harbor, Michigan, and I'll get it okay. My call's okay in the call book, too. Handle here is Jim—and you're 30 DB over S-9 here this afternoon. So, what say? W4AFV, this is W9ZZO standing by."

"W9ZZO, this is W4AFV right back. Nice transmission, Jim. Little QRM on you once, but your signal is good and steady. Say, how about the hunting and fishing out there?

If I remember right, I read an article in some magazine about Isle Royale being the 'angler's paradise.' Is that right? You know, your voice sounds familiar. Haven't I heard you playing checkers with some fellow up in Canada. Some VE? By golly, I believe you're the guy! I'm going to keep the transmissions short, Jim, cause I don't want to fade out on you. Never know when the old band will take a dive! How about it? Are you the checker player? W9ZZO, this is W4AFV standing by."

"W4AFV, this is W9ZZO right back. Yup—you've got me pegged, Hal. I play checkers with the fellow up in Canada quite often. You see, he's up above the Arctic Circle and is really isolated, so we have a lot in common. He's quite a guy, too, Name's Torval. Next time you hear us on playing checkers, break in. You'll get a big kick out of him. One day during a checker game he gave a yell—it's a wonder it didn't blast him off the air. The next thing I knew he came back and said QRX a minute—be right back. I couldn't imagine what had happened, so I stuck around. And guess what! When he came back on, he was out of breath. While he was thinking about his next checker move, he happened to glance out of his window and there was a great big, old polar bear waddling across the ice with one of Torval's frozen legs of beef in his jaws. Torval ran to get his gun. The bear evidently was snooping around the supply shed. Must have smelled the meat, pushed the door open and helped himself. You should have heard Torval tell about it. I got a big kick out of him. Wish I'd had a tape recorder! Well, anyway, Hal, next time you hear Torval and me on, be sure to break in. You'll like him. About all he does is ham. Only gets mail three times a year up there. They drop it in to him from the mail plane. He has to go by dogsled to the nearest trading post. It's not quite that bad here . . . at least, we are only isolated for the winter months. Well, Hal, I've been pretty long-winded. I'd like to stick around longer, but have some work to do on the rig, so guess I'd better say '73' and hope to see you again soon. W4AFV, this is W9ZZO standing by for your final."

"W4AFV returning, Roger, there, Jim—" The sound of a chuckle came from the speaker. "Sure would have liked to have seen that ol' bear waddlin' across the ice with that beef leg in his mouth!" Jim grinned to himself as he listened intently. "Well, I've lots of work to do, too, so we'll see you again. Thanks for the swell QSO and 73 to you, too. W9ZZO, this is W4AFV signing off and clear."

"Break! Break!"

The sharp, demanding call came on the same frequency that Hal had just signed on.

Jim flipped the transmit switch fast. "You calling W9ZZO?"

"Yes, sir! This is Marine Mobile W2NTY, aboard the freighter *Edmonson,* off the coast of Florida. How do you copy? Break—"

"Break—I copy you fine. Anything wrong? You sound desperate!" Jim leaned over the desk now, his hand on the band-spread dial, ready to follow the incoming signal if need be.

"I'll say I'm desperate! Our ship-to-shore transmitter went out a few minutes ago, as I was getting it fired up, and I can't get clearance from Tampa. We left there with a load of sulphur and by the time I got the load checked and the report made out, the transmitter went on the fritz. Any chance of getting that Tampa station back again? I heard you mention W4AFV—I can't get on 75 meters with this ham rig. Over."

Jim answered fast. "Hang on—I'll see. Calling W4AFV, W4AFV, W4AFV—hey, Hal, are you still around? Emergency! This is W9ZZO standing by."

For a moment there was nothing but the crackle of static and a heterodyne or two slightly off frequency, then— "Yup, this is W4AFV. Was just about to turn off the rig. What's up?"

"QRX a minute, will you, Hal? There's a Marine Mobile having some kind of transmitter trouble out in the Gulf and he wants to get a message into Tampa. QRX one—W2NTY-Marine Mobile, do you copy? I have Tampa standing by. Go ahead."

"W9ZZO, this is W2NTY, Marine Mobile. Brother! You sure saved my bacon, ol' man—this report has to be filed. Will you have W4AFV call our main office, Gulf Shipping Company, Magnolia 8-9595—and tell them that the transmitter burned out a transformer? I'll have it replaced within an hour, if that's all that went haywire. Tell them I'll call on the hour if and when I get it fixed. W2NTY standing by."

"Okay. QRX. W4AFV, do you copy?"

"Roger. Go ahead, Jim."

"Call Magnolia 8-9595, that's the Gulf Shipping Company, and tell them that their freighter, *Edmonson,* has transmitter trouble; burned out a transformer for one thing, and they will be on as soon as the radio operator can replace it and check the transmitter. He will call them on the hour. Over."

"Will do. Anything else?"

"Nothing else, Hal. And thanks a lot. W2NTY can

thank you when he gets back to Tampa next trip. See you later. W2NTY do you copy?"

"Sure do, go ahead."

"W4AFV will make the call right away for you, ol' man. I told him you'd thank him in person on your next trip to Tampa."

"I sure will. Kind of a long way round, but I sure appreciate your help. Glad I've got this home-brewed rig aboard, too. It's a good rig in an emergency. By the way, haven't I worked you before? W9ZZO, this is W2NTY, Marine Mobile aboard the freighter *Edmonson*, in the Gulf of Mexico, standing by."

"W9ZZO right back. Yes, I checked the log and I worked you about two months ago, Norm—that's your handle, isn't it? Remember—you were loaded with molasses and I talked to the captain that day?"

"That's right. I checked the log, too. Thought your voice sounded familiar. Well, Jim, guess I'd better get on the stick and get that transformer replaced. Hope there's nothing else wrong. And many thanks for your help. Maybe I can do something for you some time. This is W2NTY, Marine Mobile, signing off and clear. See you later."

"Keep 'em floating, Norm," Jim replied. "See you soon. W9ZZO, Isle Royale in Lake Superior, signing and pulling the big switch!"

Jim slid the station radio log toward him and began to write. Each station contacted must be written in the log, with the time called and the time contact terminated, the frequency used and the address of the station worked. In the space under REMARKS—Jim wrote—Norm burned out transformer. W4AFV called main office—relayed by me.

He pushed the completed logbook aside and leaned back in his chair. From the door of the shack he could see the back porch of the St. Cyr log cabin and the side of the root cellar, where all the winter provisions were kept.

His thoughts were jolted rudely by his nine-year-old brother, Jack, calling Charles to help him. "We've got dishes to do. Hurry up!"

Jim could see Jack as he stood at the sink, beneath the kitchen window, his sleeves rolled to his elbows, dark hair tousled and a frown wrinkling his tanned forehead. Jim knew how Jack hated the job he was doing and a grin chased away the gloom as he listened to Chuck's answer.

"I'm coming," the six-year-old called in a high-pitched, childish voice. Sounds of whistling followed this promise. Strains of *God Bless America* grew loud and clear.

Just outside the kitchen door, the whistling stopped and then Jim heard, "Now, Hill Billy, you can't come inside. I have to do my work before I can feed you. Be a good squirrel and get off my shoulder. You can sit on the window sill and watch me through the screen."

Jim saw Chuck carefully lift his pet squirrel, Hill Billy, from his shoulder, stand on tiptoe and place him on the broad ledge of the window.

"Stay there now. Just when I'm having the most fun I always hear 'DISHES'!" Chuck mimicked his older brother's voice as he skipped into the kitchen.

Latching the door of his radio shack, Jim walked slowly up the path to the cabin.

As he entered the kitchen, Jack was saying, "Gee, think we'll ever get through with these darned old dishes?" His hazel eyes dreamily contemplated a bright future with no dishes in it. "Seems like every time I turn around there's a stack of them waiting for us."

Jim answered, "Aw, quit griping and hurry up. Dad'll be here anytime now." The late sunset glowed through the sparkling windowpane and brought out the sharp contrast between the three brothers. Jim, a long-legged, red-headed, six-footer; Jack, dark-haired and hazel-eyed; Chuck, fair, with a twinkling amber glint in his deep blue, thickly lashed eyes.

"It won't take us long. There're only a few left to do," Jack told his older brother.

A scratching noise on the screen above the sink attracted Jim's attention and he waved a stern finger vaguely in Hill Billy's direction. "Sit down and keep quiet. Chuck has to finish his work!"

The squirrel evidently was used to waiting on the window ledge for Chuck. He chattered noisily as he whisked back and forth.

Jim poked at the fire in the kitchen range. His father's supper simmered in a pot on the back of the stove. Being a Forest Ranger sometimes had its advantages but Mr. St. Cyr had trained his boys well and could always count on a good meal when he came in late. Jim lifted the cover of the pot and sniffed the appetizing puffs of steam as they curled up around his face. "If I wasn't so darn full, I'd have some more of this mulligan," he said. "By the way, did they send the nuts over with the rest of the supplies?" He turned his head and twitched one eyebrow at his brother.

"Yeah," Jack answered, "the men put them in the root

house—three bushels of peanuts, five bushels of walnuts and I think they said five bushels of acorns."

"I didn't hear them come up from the Lake. What time was it?" Jim never heard much that went on outside the shack when he was talking to his radio friends.

"Oh, I don't know exactly," Jack muttered, "maybe two hours ago." A dish clattered from his hand onto the drainboard.

Chuck turned to Jim, frowning in deep concentration, "I can't understand why God didn't make some nut trees here on Isle Royale for the squirrels."

"Well—" Jim took a deep breath. He was used to Chuck's questions and knew that he might as well give a good answer because his small brother would pester him until he did. "Dad says that long ago, before the white men came to this island, there were no squirrels here."

Chuck's eyes were round with wonder but he didn't interrupt. Between Jim and Roger, this same story had been told hundreds of times. But Chuck always acted as if he'd never heard it before.

"But how did they get here, Jim?"

"The Indians brought them to Isle Royale." Jim hesitated, then gave an "Oh, well" shrug. "The Indians used to trade over on the mainland and one of them saw a pair of tame squirrels at the trading post and swopped a stack of beaver pelts for them." He broke off with a grin. "Maybe Dad'll tell you the story before you go to bed tonight."

"Golly!" was all Chuck could think of to say. "Golly!"

Jack put the last dish on the drainboard with a sigh of relief. "There!" he exclaimed and, as Jim grinned at him, he announced, "The new teacher came over today. Wonder what she's like?"

Jim snorted disgustedly. "If she's like all the others, it's going to be pretty dull. It's bad enough being stranded on this island for a whole winter without having to listen to some old sour-puss! I sure wish I could go to Houghton to school. I'm glad I graduate in June."

Jim's discontented voice evidently startled Jack and he looked at his older brother in surprise. "I never heard you talk like that before, Jim. What's wrong?"

But Jim had control of his tongue now. He hadn't meant to blurt out his dissatisfaction. Somehow, it had slipped out before he knew it. "Oh, forget it, kid. I'm going outside to wait for Dad." He slammed the kitchen door noisily behind him.

"Be with you in a sec, Jim. Almost through, Chuck?" Jack asked.

"Um-hum," mumbled the six-year-old as he made a face at himself in the shiny bottom of the pan he was wiping.

Jim slumped on the porch railing, watching for his father. His eyes searched the clearing. Their cabin was framed on the west, north and east by tall, dark fir trees and on the south by the icy waters of Lake Superior. He looked out over the lake. Tonight, he hated Lake Superior. "If I could only go to school at Houghton next summer," he thought, then jumped slightly when Jack bounded out of the door and sat down on the top porch step.

"How's the ship coming, kid?" Jim asked as Jack pulled a Boy Scout knife from one pocket and a knob of wood from another.

"Swell." Jack held up the shapeless mass of wood. "This is going to be a lifeboat for the deck!" He grinned.

"I've got three done already, one more to go." Long practice had made his fingers clever with the knife. Soon the clumsy knob began to take shape. The pile of shavings at his feet grew into a white mound of birch snow.

Presently Chuck stepped out on the porch and collected Hill Billy from the window sill. Jim, watching the rim of the clearing, saw the Forest Ranger first. His arms were loaded with packages.

Jim shouted. "There's Dad! Looks like he's been buying out the stores."

The two younger boys raced across the clearing to meet their father. Jim grinned to himself as he sat and waited.

"Hi, Dad!" both boys called as they ran. "Did you bring us something? Did the boat leave already? Did our packages come? What's in the box?" Scrambled questions and boys hit Roger St. Cyr at the same time, nearly knocking him off his feet.

Jim laughed as he heard his father answer.

"You young tornadoes had better take some of these packages and unwrap yourselves from my legs." Mr. St. Cyr chuckled as he freed himself from their clutches. "Jack, this big package is for you, and Chuck, here's your box. I'll carry the rest."

To Jim, alone on the porch, came the thought that perhaps he wanted too much. How could he expect to leave his father now? Although he was seventeen, he'd been his father's right-hand man for at least four years, following him around the island to check the forests and the moose herds, making radio reports to the mainland. In addition, the bookwork had to be kept up, even in the winter, when Jim had to go to school.

"Hi, Dad!" Jim called finally, when his father was half-

way across the clearing. "How was the trip? See anyone
I know?" He would have enjoyed going to the mainland
with his father on this last trip before the freeze-up.

"I saw some of the boys at the main office but that's
about all. I didn't have much time after I left the store."
Mr. St. Cyr shook his head. "Did a little shopping,
though, besides getting everything else we needed." He
looked around at the packages. "If I've forgotten anything, they'll have to drop it later by plane."

"By the look in Chuck's eyes, I can tell he's got a present of some kind!" Jim's hearty laughter broke through
and his listless mood disappeared.

Chuck, instead of talking, had been trying to unwrap
his huge box. String and wrappings followed in his wake.
Hill Billy, perching on his shoulder, scolded him for being
so untidy.

The porch was as far as the two younger boys could go
with the bundles. Their curiosity was too great. Jim and
their father chuckled as they watched them. Jack suc-
ceeded in extricating his present first and out of his package came a beautiful MacTavish plaid mackinaw, lined in
soft, scarlet wool. It had a detachable hood.

"Gee, Dad, this's super!" Jack's eyes sparkled as he
slipped into the coat. "And it's reversible, too! Golly!"

"I thought it was pretty elegant myself, Son. We'll be
able to see you coming a mile away!"

"Yippee! Jackie! Lookit!" This was Chuck. He was
up-ended into the large box, with nothing much in view
except feet and legs. By some feat of balance, his feet
were still on the floor. Sweater, shirts of bright and gaudy
plaids, boots, mittens and handkerchiefs were flying out
of the box.

"I got it! I got it! Oh, Daddy, I thought you didn't remember!"

"Remember what?" Jim was curious.

Chuck emerged with a red face and shining eyes, hands clutching a bright green, three-decked squirrel cage.

He inspected every nook and cranny of the carefully built house, then each of the boys in turn had to examine and rave over it.

"Now I suppose I won't have a minute's rest till I build him half a dozen more just like it," Jack protested to Jim, then turned to his own large bundle. "Mitts, socks, hankies, shirts, underwear, Jiminy! Dad, you didn't forget a thing, did you? What's this package on the bottom?" Jack dug down into the box while Jim and Chuck leaned over to see better.

As Jack unwrapped the package, Jim could see the little smile curve softly around the corners of his brother's mouth and detect the eager wish in his eyes. At last the package was free of its wrappings and there, glinting in the setting sun, was a beautiful set of wood carving knives in three different sizes, plus a scout hatchet and hunting knife.

Jack's voice caught in his throat as he cried, "Gee, Dad!" He hesitated, "It's—it's simply super duper!"

Mr. St. Cyr smiled. "Now you can whittle to your heart's content, but be doggone careful because they're plenty sharp. We don't want any whittled fingers!"

"There was a message for you late this afternoon from the mainland, Dad," Jim said. "I told the radio operator that you'd gone over on the boat for supplies and wouldn't be back till late, so he gave it to me. Good thing I've got my radio operator's license."

"It's been a great help, Jim." Mr. St. Cyr put his arm around his son's shoulders and gave him a brief squeeze. "What did they want?"

"The Conservation Department wants to round up a hundred moose. They're going to take them to the mainland, to the Cusino Game Refuge, for the winter. Then they won't have to bring over so much feed. Last year, too many cows and calves died to suit them, I guess. They said they're sending some men over on a Coast Guard cutter to help round the moose up."

"I wonder what they'll think up next," Mr. St. Cyr murmured. "How they're ever going to round up a bunch of jittery moose is more than I can figure out. Is that all they said?"

"They said they'd send a boat over later, to transport them to the mainland." Jim answered.

"That means we'll be plenty busy for a while at any rate. But rounding up moose! Humph!" The Forest Ranger snorted. "Anything else?"

Jim raised an eyebrow. "He asked if the warehouse was ready for the hay they're shipping over and if the bins are ready for the other feed for the moose."

"Of course, you told them they've been ready for months, didn't you?" Roger St. Cyr asked as he moved toward the kitchen door.

"Sure." Jim followed his father.

Jack and Chuck were running toward the Lake now, to watch the men unload supplies from the small Diesel boat.

"Fine. Now all we have to do is see that the men don't starve when they get here." The Ranger walked over to the stove and lifted the lid off the kettle of stew. "Boy, oh, boy, this certainly smells scrumptious!" He sniffed cautiously, "What is it?"

"Better not let Jack hear you ask that, Dad!" Jim laughed, "He made it—and, it's darn good, too!" He reached for the bubbling coffeepot and poured Mr. St. Cyr a cup of steaming coffee. "I might even have another helping with you."

"Swell," Mr. St. Cyr chuckled as he dished out a big ladleful for himself and held out his hand for his son's plate. "By the way, Jim," he turned with the full plate in his hand, "I got those traps you wanted. They must be out in the warehouse. They were somewhere in the boat with the rest of the supplies."

"Did I give you enough money for them or have they raised the ante since last fall?" Jim settled himself at the kitchen table and waited for his father to answer.

"You gave me plenty. In fact, I think there was about four bucks left, so I got you that radio oscillator you wanted." Roger St. Cyr tasted his stew eagerly, then grinned delightedly. "Jack can sure hustle up a good meal!"

But Jim wasn't interested in eating now. "Golly, Dad, did you really? I've wanted one ever since the rest of the kids on the island got theirs. But you're kidding, aren't you? There was just enough to get the traps!" Jim waited eagerly for the answer.

His father smiled understandingly at him. "Well, maybe I did stretch things a bit, but I knew you wanted one, so we'll call it quits!"

"Which means, you're about four bucks out. I know you."

"Forget it, kid," his father responded softly as he turned back to his supper.

Jim couldn't see into his father's mind just then. If he could have, he'd have seen how proud Roger St. Cyr was of his oldest son. Jim, growing tall and sturdy and with a brilliant mind, was working at his radio gadgets with a sureness that derives only from a complete knowledge of his subject. Added to that was his wizardry at trapping during the long winter months—and his rapidly mounting bank account, after the pelts were cured and traded for cash. No, Jim couldn't see all this passing through his father's mind until his chest seemed almost to burst with pride. Nor could he tell that his father always pictured him in the uniform of the Forest Ranger.

Jim wondered if this were the right time for him to mention casually again about going to summer school during the next vacation. He had been dropping hints for several months now and his father usually laughed them aside. Several times they'd had an argument about it and, so far, Mr. St. Cyr had won out. He just couldn't agree to anything that would take Jim to the mainland, even if the boy did want to study radio at the Michigan College of Mines in Houghton. Jim knew that his father was unwilling to give his consent. It was the only thing they had ever disagreed on and, since the last argument, the boy had maintained a hurt silence on the subject.

Mr. St. Cyr broke the silence first. "The new teacher came over on the boat with us today." He glanced up at his son. "She's a lot different from Miss Ward—and only about half as old! I think you'll like her."

Jim sputtered. "After Miss Ward, I think we could get

along with most anyone." He wagged his head and made a face. "Wow! She sure was an old battleax!"

Jack and Chuck heard the last part of Jim's sentence when they bounded into the kitchen with their new possessions and Jack added his two cents. "You can say that again!" He shifted several bundles he was carrying to the table. "The fellows left these other packages with the supplies. What's in them?"

"The rest of these parcels can't be opened now." Mr. St. Cyr looked at Chuck. "After the winter freeze, we won't be able to get to the mainland, so Santa Claus had to fill our orders early."

Chuck's eyes were wide and round. "Did you really see Santa Claus Pop?" He only used the word Pop when he was excited.

"I didn't see Santa, but I saw his helper." He hesitated a moment then, "Suppose you help put some of these bundles away; that is, if you think Hill Billy can spare you for a few minutes?"

"Of course, I'll help you, Pop! Hill Billy won't mind!"

"How does he like his new mansion?" the Ranger asked.

"He likes it fine!" Chuck answered. " Just wait till the other squirrels see it, I'll bet they all want to live in it!"

Jim hooted at this. "Now see what you've started, Dad! Mutiny in the squirrel colony!" While they all laughed, Jim knew that mutiny wasn't to be confined to the squirrel colony. He *must* find some way to bring up the subject tomorrow. He just had to persuade his father some way to let him go to the mainland next summer, to radio school. Some way—but how?

2

vvvvv • vvvvv • vvvvv • vvvvv • vvvvv • vvvvv • vvvvv

Jim left his father and two brothers in the kitchen. He'd heard a message coming in on the Forestry frequency and hurried in to see for whom it was intended. The Ranger radio station occupied a small, especially built room adjoining the large living room and both Jim's and his father's radio licenses hung over the operating position. A big Ranger clock was directly over the receiver. Separated from the living room by a sliding door, the radio room could be isolated from or open to the living room. Mostly, the sliding door stayed open and the receiver remained alerted on the Ranger frequency.

During the winter months, when the island was snowbound and isolated from the mainland, Mr. St. Cyr and his three boys spent many happy hours in the big living room, each with his own hobby—mostly Jack with his whittling, Chuck with Hill Billy, Jim with a textbook on radio and their father with a book and his pipe. Of course, the sliding door to the radio room was left open.

20

A few minutes later, Jim heard his father shooing the two boys to bed, and then he heard them call for him to tell them a story and tuck them in for the night. He pushed away from the radio table and sauntered into their room.

Bunk beds in the far corner were covered with gay Hudson Bay blankets, matching the scheme of the room. The windows extended across one entire side of the room and through them one could look out diagonally across the Lake. Heavy sailcloth draperies closed over the entire stretch of windows. On the right wall, as one entered the room, a large stone fireplace lent an old-fashioned air of elegance to the room. Its cheery fire now made the room bright and cozy.

Aladdin lamps were the lighting fixtures for the entire cabin and in this room a hurricane lamp had been remodeled to use the mantels of an Aladdin lamp. A generator, to supply electric power for the cabin and radio shack, had been on order for some time but had not arrived. Home-tanned skin rugs dotted the white pine, waxed floor and a huge black bear rug, trophy of a Canadian hunt, sprawled in front of the fireplace.

Jim stood in the doorway and announced, "I smell a story!"

Gleefully, Chuckie called, "Come on, Jim, Dad's just promised to tell us the story about the squirrels!" Chuckie patted the side of his bed. "Sit by me. There's lots of room."

Jim walked over to the side of the bed and sat down. "All right, Runt," he tousled Chuckie's hair until his small brother squealed for mercy.

Mr. St. Cyr made himself comfortable in a big armchair

by the glowing fire and lit his pipe. "All set?" he asked the three boys.

"Shoot!" piped up Jack, who had been hastily tumbling out of his clothes and into his pajamas.

Roger St. Cyr puffed out a fat smoke ring and began.

"Once upon a time, many, many, many years ago, there lived on Isle Royale, a tribe of Indians called the Chippewas.

"Not one of the tribe had ever seen a squirrel or even the track of one, on the island. They were very sad about this because squirrel meat was a dainty to them and the soft, fine fur was used to trim their clothes." The storyteller settled more comfortably in the huge chair.

"Trips to the mainland were planned, to trade pelts for food at the fur trading post and, one day in the late spring, after the ice had broken around the island, a dozen canoes started off with their winter catch of pelts."

Chuck interrupted the story. "Did they cross Lake Superior in a little canoe, Pop?" His face was caught in the flickering light of the fire and it showed his eyes wide with excitement.

"Certainly, that's the only kind of boat the Indians ever had. But they were skilled with a paddle and enjoyed those trips to the mainland." Mr. St. Cyr resumed his story.

"At the trading post, while the Indians were bargaining with the trader, a little girl came in with a squirrel sitting on her shoulder."

"Just like Hill Billy and me, Pop?" Chuck questioned.

"Yes, I imagine just like you. Now are you going to keep quiet while I finish the story?" His father chuckled. "Or would you rather tell me the story?"

"Not that he couldn't," Jim broke in with a laugh, "I'll bet this is the thousandth time we've heard it!"

"Okay, Pop. I'll keep still. Golly, can't a guy say anything around here?" Chuck slid down under the bedclothes until just the tip of his nose showed.

"Well," his father resumed, "when the Indians saw the animal, they asked the trader to sell them the squirrel, but the man wouldn't sell. It was the little girl's pet. But, he added, he had a colony of squirrels and he might sell them a pair from that colony. In their eagerness to secure the squirrels, each brave gave a bundle of beaver pelts to the surprised trader in exchange.

"The trader gave the Indians a cage for the two squirrels and they were taken to the island to live. But the poor creatures couldn't find much to eat, for there were no nut trees on the island, with the exception of hazelnut bushes. Finally, the squirrels grew so thin that the braves held a powwow!" Mr. St. Cyr stopped to relight his pipe.

"So," Chuck instinctively continued the story, "early the next morning a canoe set out for another trip to the mainland and late that night it came back loaded with big bundles of nuts of all kinds. From then on, the Indians had to feed the squirrels by hand and that's why the ones on this island are so tame!"

"See," Jim joked, "he even uses your words, Dad!" He got up from Chuck's bed. "Night, kids. Sleep tight!"

Jack and Chuck called sleepily, "Night, Jim!"

Mr. St. Cyr soon joined his son in the living room. The boy had dropped down in front of the fireplace and his gaze was held, as if by hypnotic power, by the sparks and flickering flames that danced in the updraft.

Better not stay up very late tonight, Jim," his father advised. "If it's nice tomorrow, we may have our last picnic before school starts."

"Where to?" Jim broke his rapt gaze into the fire and looked at his father.

"I have to take a trip up to Moose Lake and we might as well make it a picnic. We can look around for the moose herd at the same time." Mr. St. Cyr turned out the lights and threw another log on the bright coals in the fireplace.

Jim's thoughts weren't on picnics or the moose herd, in fact, he hadn't heard much of the squirrel story. He was too busy thinking of a way to convince his dad that he really must go to radio school. He turned around on one elbow and looked up at his father. Now might be a good time, he thought, and was about to speak when the Ranger said, "Good night, Jim."

"Good night, Dad," Jim answered slowly and turned back to stare again into the fire.

The next morning dawned bright, cold and clear, with a tang in the air. Frost crystals on the grass blades sparkled in the sunlight. The smoke from the fireplace in the big living room rose straight into the crackling air and, in the distance, the bawling of a moose calf echoed and re-echoed through the forest.

Jim was frying strips of bacon and setting the break-fast table while Mr. St. Cyr stirred up a batch of pancakes. The two younger boys were scampering in and out of the kitchen.

"Something smells awful good out there," Jack yelled

from the bedroom, "Make plenty of whatever it is. Boy! Am I hungry!"

"Me, too, Pop," chimed in Chuck as he struggled half in and half out of his sweater. "What's cookin'?"

Jim lifted a heaping platter of bacon from the warming oven and carried it quickly over to the table. "Bacon— come an' get it!" he answered.

His father began to dish up pancakes into a golden mound on a huge platter. "Dig in; we want to get started soon. It's quite a hike up to Moose Lake." He pulled his chair away from the table and sat down. "I think we'd better look over the trap trails that are on our way, too. We can expect snow any day now."

Jim stated between mouthfuls of pancake, "It sure smells like winter this morning. Only fifty degrees at seven o'clock, but the sun'll warm it up a little." He turned to his father, "Shall I take the radio transceiver, Dad?"

"We probably won't need it but if you want to bother with it, that's okay with me." Mr. St. Cyr turned to caution the younger boys. "You'd better dress warmly. It may even snow before we get back tonight. I'll put up the lunch while you get out your warmer clothes. What'll it be? Hot dogs or hamburgers?"

"I don't care what it is as long as there's lots of it. Anything tastes like caviar out in the woods!" Jack smacked his lips in an exaggerated way.

"How do you know what caviar tastes like?" Jim teased. "You've never had any."

"Well, I can read, can't I, and that's what they always say in books. 'Champagne and caviar!' Now if they'd say, 'Ham and eggs'—that's something else again."

"You fellows dress good and warm. We won't be back much before dark tonight and you'll need all your heavy stuff on," admonished Mr. St. Cyr once again. "You can try out some of your new duds!"

By the time the boys had donned their new winter clothes, Mr. St. Cyr had the lunch packed in a large basket. Ham sandwiches, jelly sandwiches, peanut butter sandwiches, hamburger buns and hamburger, ready to pop into the frying pan. Pickles and hard-boiled eggs, butter cookies that Jack had made just a few days before and a large thermos bottle filled with hot chocolate and one of coffee.

Jim was ready first. "Where in heck do you think we're going, Dad? You've got enough to eat for a week!" He lifted the basket and groaned.

"That's what you think. Coming home that basket'll be empty, or practically, anyway." His father laughed. "If I'm not right, I'll eat the basket."

The boys giggled and Jim answered. "A fine picture that'll make!" Then more seriously, he asked, "What do we have to take a look at the moose herd for, Dad? You checked them over about a week ago."

"If those fellows are coming over to round up moose, we've got to tell them where they are. They could hunt for weeks and never find them."

"Well, I guess we're all ready then, Dad. Let's get a move on!" Jim slipped the transceiver straps over his shoulder and hoisted the case to his back. Maybe, today, he thought, I can talk Dad into letting me go to Houghton next summer, to radio school.

3

vvvv • vvvv • vvvv • vvvv • vvvv • vvvv • vvvv

The trip to Moose Lake would ordinarily be made in about two and a half hours of steady walking, but today, Ranger St. Cyr and the three boys, all loaded down with packs of various kinds, took their time.

Deer poked wet, shining noses through the green foliage. Rabbits hopped across the trail, practically underfoot. Squirrels, evidently descendants of the original pair brought to the island by the Indians, chattered at each other and scampered from treetop to treetop, always with one eye on the trail below.

Black and red fox slyly peered from behind windfalls, not afraid, yet not bold. Slant-eyed lynx slipped through the dense forest underbrush, curious and alert.

Jim, ahead on the trail, watched for familiar landmarks.

Suddenly he stopped and pointed, "Look, Chuck, there's Shadow! See him up in that dead tree?"

"Golly," Chuck answered, "I haven't seen him since last week. He must have been away visiting. He stole a lot of nuts out of the storehouse." He chuckled when he remembered how he had caught the sly squirrel. "I saw him hauling them out when the men were unloading supplies."

A little later, Jim called. "There's Bambino. He doesn't stay around much now. He must have a family."

The boys looked ahead and there, on the path in front of them, stood the deer that Ranger St. Cyr had taken care of two winters before, when it broke its leg. A sunburst of tan on his deep white chest identified him to them.

When the group started on again, Bambino merely crossed the trail majestically and stood watching them out of sight.

Bright, rainbow-colored birds sang noisily to each other and darted in and out, just over the travelers' heads. Jim looked up from time to time and whistled peculiar calls to them. On the trapping trails, he had perfected many bird calls, so never felt alone in the deep woods.

Keenly aware of their animal friends, the St. Cyrs continued their trek. Now and then, Jim would call out and everyone would stop, put down his load and rest, while Jim followed a faint track into the thick underbrush. Returning, he'd generally blaze a tree near the trail. His system of blazing was one he had perfected himself. A straight slash meant "trail okay for traps;" a cross meant "change traps for different animal," a star meant "abandon trail."

But through all the trail blazing and tramping up the trail, one thing ran continually through Jim's mind. I hope I can talk to Dad some time today!

By the time they were approaching the lake, they had

fifteen or twenty new trails located. Of course, all of these might not be good for trapping, but that would only be known after they had been tried for a week or so.

Suddenly Jim stopped in the trail and put up his hand. "We're getting near the lake," he called back to his father, who was last in line. "I can hear the moose now, Listen! Can't you?"

The Ranger hesitated, his head turned slightly. "There seem to be a lot of tracks around here. The herd can't be very far away."

Jim shifted his pack to his other shoulder. "We'll have to go along carefully. The herd will get nervous, if they're surprised. Don't want any tree climbing today. It's too cold." When Jack and Chuck snickered, Jim looked around at the tall spruce and pine trees. "Besides, who wants to climb a Christmas tree?"

By now Mr. St. Cyr had walked up to where Jim stood. "We'll have to branch off the main trail here and circle them so they won't catch our scent," he said. "When we get down wind from them, they won't smell us."

Looking skyward, he observed the wind direction to be northeast by the bend of the limber treetops, so he led the boys off the trail to the northwest.

They had only gone a few steps off trail when Jim warned sharply, "Be darn careful, kids. I nearly fell into a mining pit. You can't see them till you're right on top of them."

"Don't slip on these rocks either," his father called back. "The underbrush is pretty thick, so watch your step!"

"Okay, Pop," Chuck answered staunchly. "We'll watch

out for them." And Hill Billy, perched on his shoulder chattered back noisily.

It was now only a short distance to the lake, and as the four broke through the dense growth at the edge of the clearing, they could see the moose herd on the other side of the lake, moving heavily, slowly, in and out of the trees, wallowing in the deep mud at the edge of the water.

Some of the cows and calves were standing shoulder deep among the lily pads, others were drinking nearer shore. All of them possessed a quiet dignity. On a knoll, outlined against the blue sky, stood the sentinel moose, its huge antlered head raised high as it swung slowly from side to side, sniffing the pure air.

The sight of the moose always gave Jim a sense of his own smallness, and today, as he stood there watching these huge creatures browse, he felt like a midget. Calves waded in the boggy lake and nibbled at the tender water lily seedlings. Yellow cow lilies were a delicacy, too, and only those hidden by logs and brush were protected from the raiders.

Jim dropped the heavy pack from his back. "My arms are aching, Dad. How about making camp here?" He rubbed his arms briskly and swung them around in the air to take the kinks out of his muscles.

"I guess this is as good a place as any," his father answered as he followed Jim's example. "We can find some wood and, after the moose see us, they won't care whether we're here or not."

Jim turned to his brothers, who stood watching the moose across the lake. "You kids find some wood for the fire. I'll build up an oven with some of these rocks." He kicked at a large stone with his toe. "I slipped in a few potatoes to stick in the coals!"

"Yum! Yum!" Chuck licked his lips. "Am I ever hungry."

While the two younger boys hunted for wood, Jim built a small oven out of rocks and in a few minutes the fire was burning brightly in the outdoor stove. Ranger St. Cyr unstrapped the camp grill, a companion on many of these trips, and soon a tantalizing odor of hamburgers, charred potatoes and wieners filled the air.

The sentinel moose, obviously, had long since seen the party and, after a few snorts to put the rest of the herd at ease, had turned to the more important business of feeding. Large bass and yellow-bellied perch leaped high out of the water, feeding on flies, or perhaps just for sport. Several beaver were busily carrying twigs and limbs from the forest's edge to their colony underwater. An occasional slap of a beaver tail on top of the water sounded like a pistol shot.

"We've never camped at exactly this spot before, have we, Dad?" Jim asked as the two younger boys stood near, sniffing the good food smells and watching the animal activity.

"No, I don't think we have," his father answered slowly. "After dinner you fellows," he nodded at Jack and Chuck, "can scout around. It's just possible that you might find some arrowheads for your collection. There're lots of those shallow pits around here, though, so, for the love of Mike, be careful!"

Jim, busy spreading out the remaining contents of the picnic hamper, turned and asked over his shoulder, "How soon'll the spuds be done, Dad? Everything here's ready and waiting."

Mr. St. Cyr poked the end of a long, pointed stick he'd whittled into the center of the fire and speared a potato on the end of it. It seemed to be cooked through. "They should be about ready," he declared. "I boiled them for fifteen minutes with their jackets on this morning, so they wouldn't take so long to bake."

"Come on, kids. By the time you load your plates up, the Murphys'll be done." Jim handed Chuck a heaping plate and asked, "There, fellow, how does that look?"

As the youngest St. Cyr nodded and took the heaping plate, you could almost see his mouth water. Soon he was too busy to bother with an answer.

Later, after everyone had eaten all they could hold, the two younger boys scrambled up the rocky slope toward the forest. Jack took several photographs of the moose herd from various angles and Chuck watched him without talking.

"They sure won't be hungry for a little while," Jim laughed as he scraped the few leftover scraps into the glowing coals. The splatter of grease sounded like tiny firecrackers. "Hadn't we better call Copper Harbor and tell them that we've located the herd and find out when they plan to come over?"

Mr. St. Cyr puffed vigorously at his briar pipe. "It wouldn't be a bad idea. I told them last night that I wouldn't call them today 'til we'd located the herd. Yes —call them." He pushed his heavy plaid cap far back on his head and brushed a stray, wavy lock from his forehead.

It took but a minute for Jim to pull out the antenna

and flip the switch of the transceiver, to warm up the tubes. Then he said evenly, "Portable WRR, Isle Royale, calling WZZ, Copper Harbor and standing by."

"WRR/portable, Isle Royale—this is WZZ, Copper Harbor," came back through the loudspeaker. "Have been listening for your call. Did you find the herd? Copper Harbor WZZ over."

Jim handed the microphone to his father.

"WZZ this is WRR—portable at Copper Harbor. Roger St. Cyr speaking. Yes, we're at Moose Lake and the herd is here. There seems to be a lot of good browse left, although they've cleaned out most of the water and cow lily pads. We're on the northwest end of the lake and there's very little ground hemlock here. Pretty well browsed or trampled, perhaps both. Sedge mat vegetation churned up and broken off around the whole lake edge. Guess that's all. When are we to expect the men? WRR over."

"Copper Harbor to Isle Royale. Thanks, Roger, for the dope. The men should be over some time next week. We have to finish the pens first. That's all for today. Have a good time. WZZ, Copper Harbor off and clear with WRR, portable Isle Royale. So long."

"Good-by. See you tomorrow." Roger St. Cyr flipped the switch to "off" and handed the microphone back to Jim. "Well, that's that." He nodded.

Jim had just taken the microphone from his father's hand when a bloodcurdling yell made him jump and almost drop it. "What the deuce was that?" His eyebrows shot skyward and he turned around with a jerk.

Mr. St. Cyr leaped up and started on a run in the direction of the scream. Rocks rolled and slipped beneath their feet as they raced up the steep slope toward the spot where Jack and Chuck had vanished into the thick underbrush.

Before they could reach the top of the slope, Chuck came crying out of the woods. "Daddy! Daddy!" He sobbed hysterically. "Jackie fell in a big hole and can't get out. I think he's hurt 'cause he won't talk to me."

Jim took the frightened little boy by the shoulders and shook him gently. "Where is he? Hurry!" Soon, with Chuck leading them, Jim and his father reached the spot where Jack had disappeared. Ground pine and brush had made a thick screen over the opening of the hole. Evidently Jack had not followed the trail because it was off to one side. Luckily, the pit was a shallow one, not over ten feet deep, and the brush had broken the boy's fall.

As they peered over the edge, Jack stirred and moaned. His father called down to him, "Jack! Jack! Are you hurt badly?"

Jim stripped off his heavy coat and pulled off his scout belt. "Take hold of this, Dad. I'll climb down after him. I can get down there better than you can." Jim's mind worked with lightning speed in any emergency.

His father grasped the end of the belt and wound it around his hand. "Okay, Jim. Over you go and for heaven's sake be careful!" He braced himself against the sudden jerk.

Jim's feet cautiously found footholds in the rocky side of the pit and in a moment he was down on his knees at Jack's side. A rock had cut a long gash in the boy's forehead and blood spurted from the open wound every time his heart pumped. Jim's skilled fingers sought and found the exact spot where pressure would shut off the heavy

flow of blood. One of his Eagle Scout accomplishments
had helped him again.

"Dad," he called up, "I've got to have some bandages.
Hurry! He's lost a lot of blood." His other hand explored
Jack's arms and legs but could find no broken bones.

"Here's the kit, Jim," his father called as he tossed the
tin carefully down to the floor of the pit. "Think you can
handle him?"

"I think so. He's coming around now. Jack! Jack! Can
you hear me?" Jim's voice urged as he quickly and effi-
ciently bandaged his brother's head.

A groan and then Jack's eyes opened. "Wh-what happened?" he muttered. Gradually the dazed expression
left his eyes. "I sure—put my—foot in it that time, eh,
Jim?" He grinned feebly.

"Sure, you'll be okay, but take it easy for a minute,"
Jim insisted. "What kind of a stunt did you think you
were pulling off?"

"The darned old hole was covered and I didn't even
see it! I was backing up, trying to take a picture of a
red-headed woodpecker up in that tree." Jack made a
move to sit up but groaned and fell back into Jim's arms.
"My head's going round—"

"You'll be all right in a minute. Just take it easy. Here,"
Jim slid an arm under his brother's shoulder, "lean on me
and we'll have you out of here in a jiffy."

Jack sighed. "Wouldn't you know I'd do something
like this?" He struggled to sit up again and this time was
able to hold his head up without feeling too faint.

"How do you feel?" Jim asked after a moment. "Think
you can stand up now?"

"Sure. But my leg kind of hurts." Jack rubbed his left

leg and started to stand. "Maybe I'm wrong, but I think I broke something, Jim. It's beginning to hurt like the dickens!"

"It doesn't seem to be broken," Jim muttered as his fingers again explored for possible injuries. "But," he hesitated a bit, "it's starting to swell. Dad, give us a hand. I think he's sprained his ankle!"

It took the combined efforts of Mr. St. Cyr and Chuck and Jim to get Jack out of the hole and by the time they had him out on the ground, his ankle had swollen to double its size. Jim and his father made a seat with their hands and carried the boy back to the campfire.

"I'll bind this so it won't swell any more. Think you can take it, kid?" Jim asked as he slit Jack's heavy breeches. The flesh underneath was rapidly turning black and blue where he had banged it against the rocks in his fall.

"I—I guess so." A tear rolled down Jack's cheek. "But take it easy, eh?"

While Jim wrapped Jack's leg, their father was studying the sky.

"We'll be lucky to get home before it snows. The sky looks pretty black over in the northeast," he said, turning back to the boys. "That wind might blow up a nice little flurry. We'd better get started."

"How're we going to carry him, Dad? Think we can make a seat?" Jim knew that it was going to be tough, getting Jack back to the cabin. Besides being a long hike, it was going to jar that hurt leg, but there was nothing else to do.

"I'll carry the transceiver, Jim," Ranger St. Cyr said quietly so that Jack couldn't hear, "and we'll just have to take our time. The only thing that worries me is that he might faint from pain and loss of blood before we get him back. . . . Here, Chuck, you can carry the basket. It's a good thing it's almost empty. I'll put out the fire." He stopped short. "Oh-Oh!" he mumbled, "we're in for it, all right!" He held up his arm and looked at the star-like crystal drop nestled in the woolly fuzz. "These clouds are moving fast. We'd better make tracks!"

Although it was only two o'clock in the afternoon, the sky was already beginning to darken.

Jim and his father struggled along with Jack between them, seated on their hands.

The trail was rocky and, although Jack was silent, Jim knew that he was suffering with every step they took.

It was getting harder to see the trail and they bent low to protect their faces from the sharp, icy flakes. Chuck, walking behind them with the picnic basket, had trouble keeping up with them. It was beginning to snow harder now and talking was impossible.

"Gee, Dad," Jim said finally, "I'll have to rest a minute. My hands are so numb I can't hang onto yours any longer. We can let Jack sit on the picnic hamper, can't we?"

"Sure! Chuck, bring it here," Ranger St. Cyr called and his son hurried forward with the empty basket.

They put Jack down gently. His face was drawn and pale and there was blood on his lower lip from biting it to smother groans. Jim looked at his father over Jack's head and frowned. If they didn't get him back to the cabin soon, loss of blood from his head wound might cause serious complications. The awkwardness of walking and carrying the injured boy between them jolted him with every step and Jim noticed a fresh bloodstain seeping through the thick bandage he'd put on Jack's head.

"Let's go, and we'd better hurry!" Jim urged and, once more, he locked hands with his father. This time Jack couldn't help himself much and Jim knew that they wouldn't be able to stop again until they reached the cabin. He wondered if he could make it.

They plodded on through the deepening snow. Chuck hung on to the back of his father's coat, so that he could keep up. The pace had been terrific for him.

On and on they trudged. The trail seemed endless to Jim who, by now, was numb clear to his shoulders . . . but he knew he must keep on. They must get Jack to the cabin. When they finally reached the clearing, he was ready to scream. The numbness was turning to fire now and his arms protested with sharp, angry stabs of pain. Jack was in a half faint, one arm around his father's neck, the other dangling limply at his side.

When they entered the cabin it seemed like heaven. The fire in the fireplace had about burned itself out, but, with a little coaxing, it would soon burn brightly again. Mr. St. Cyr took Jack in his arms and laid him carefully down on his bed, while Jim threw another big log on the fire and ran for the first-aid kit.

"We'll need some hot water and more bandages, Jim," the Ranger said as he cut away the bandana handkerchief he'd used for a makeshift binder. "This doesn't look too good!"

"Poor kid, he certainly didn't have much fun today!" Jim spoke low but Jack heard him and opened his eyes.

"Oh heck, I'll be okay—in the morning—" he said faintly but his brother knew that he was hurt worse than he realized.

Jim dressed Jack's leg again and put a fresh bandage on his head while their father fixed a bowl of hot milk for the invalid.

After they had made Jack comfortable for the night, Mr. St. Cyr patted him on the head and whispered, "Good night, soldier!" then left the darkened room quietly.

Jim tucked the covers snugly about his brother's shoulders and murmured, "G'night, kid. Take it easy. You'll be okay now!" He slipped quietly out after his father, closing the door almost shut, so the light from the kitchen wouldn't disturb the patient.

4

vvvv • vvvv • vvvv • vvvv • vvvv • vvvv • vvvv

Next morning, Jim was the first one up. He peeked in to see if Jack was awake but steady breathing from both boys told him they were still asleep. As he turned from the door, his father pushed past him into the darkened room, to stand over the sleeping boys. Shortly afterwards, he joined Jim in the kitchen. Over toast and coffee, they talked in low voices.

"Golly, I could hardly get to sleep last night," Jim sighed as he riffled his uncombed, red hair. "My arms ached all night. It's a good thing we didn't have any farther to go. I sure was pooped!"

"Don't think I escaped either. This morning my arms feel as if they'd been hammered with a mallet!" The Ranger grinned over his steaming coffee cup. He was scheduled for a trip up the coast and, if he didn't get started soon, it would be late afternoon before he could get back.

"Dad," Jim began slowly, "about school!" He looked at his father a bit cautiously, to see his reaction.

Avoiding a reply, Mr. St. Cyr reminded him, "Take good care of Jack today. Don't let him get up. I'll be back as soon as I can."

"Dad," Jim spoke insistently now. "How about school?"

"Well?" Mr. St. Cyr asked. "What about it?"

Jim saw the line around his father's mouth tighten and knew he'd better not mention his ambitions now. "Oh, nothing. I might take a run down to see if the new teacher is there." He passed the remark off, then pushed his chair away from the table. "Do you know what time you'll be back?"

Evidently his father was relieved when Jim didn't mention radio school, because the tight line faded from his lips and a smile quirked at their corners. "About lunch time. And give the new teacher my regards." Roger lifted one eyebrow quizzically at his handsome son and made a remark that Jim thought was very strange, coming from his father. "She's quite a dish!"

"Oh, oh!" Jim choked on a piece of toast, "don't tell me you've got a crush on the new teacher! She really must be *some* dish!"

His father patted vaguely at his mouth with his napkin. "Don't be juvenile, Jim! I mean she's quite a change from the others we've had."

"She must be," Jim teased. He looked at his watch. "Gosh, I've got to rush! I've got a sked with Tom. See you later, Dad."

"Take good care of Jack," Mr. St. Cyr admonished again. "He'll be okay but don't let him get out of bed. He was asleep when I looked in a few minutes ago. If you leave the cabin, don't be gone for long. I expect some more dope from the mainland on the herders." He buttoned his heavy jacket and looked into his lunch pail, to see what Jim had been putting into it.

Jim called "Okay" from the edge of the porch and then raced up the trail to the radio shack. As he pushed open the door, he glanced at his watch. It was almost time for his schedule on 75 meters with W9ZZY on Devil's Island. He flipped switches automatically and watched the filaments heat to a bright red. Signals began to crackle from the loudspeaker and he turned the dial to 3924, the frequency he usually worked Jerry on.

Jerry was a member of the Coast Guard on Devil's Island, one of the Apostle Islands at the western end of Lake Superior. Located about eighteen miles by water from Bayfield, Wisconsin, the island was a guardian of the upbound and downbound freighters that plied Lake Superior, bringing cargoes from the lower lakes. Manned by four, sometimes five men, the Devil's Island Radio Beacon gave lake traffic the fix the ships needed to keep on course.

"Calling W9ZZO, W9ZZO, W9ZZO. This is W9ZZY, Devil's Island in Lake Superior calling and standing by. What say, Jim, you around?"

Jim's hands were expert as he turned on the final of his transmitter. "W9ZZY, this is W9ZZO, Isle Royale calling. Do you copy? Over."

"Thought you weren't going to make it. This is W9ZZY. I was almost ready to call CQ, thought maybe you got tied up. What's new?"

"W9ZZY, this is W9ZZO. I didn't realize what time it was. Nothing much new around here except we got word from the mainland that we're going to be chasing moose pretty soon. How do you like that?"

"Chasing moose? Who you trying to kid?"

"Honest! That's what I said . . . chasing moose! Cow pokes will be over to round up some of the moose herd. They want to move them so they won't starve this winter. But how they're going to do it is what I'm wondering."

"Now I've heard everything! Wish I could come over and watch the fun. Say, I talked to Katchy this morning. They were just leaving Duluth. He wondered where you've been keeping yourself. I told him to listen for us this morning and break in if he heard us. Over."

"9ZZY, this is W9ZZO, Isle Royale. Fine business. I haven't talked to Katchy since he changed ships. I haven't even heard him. What ship's he on? Over."

"He's on the *S. S. Norcliff*—carrying grain and rock from Duluth. Let's see if he's around. W8XI/Marine Mobile, W8XI, W8XI . . . W9ZZY and W9ZZO are standing by for you. What say?"

"W9ZZY, W9ZZO, this is W8XI/Marine Mobile right back. Yup, I've been monitoring your frequency for the last half hour, while I did some paper work. Got a load of grain aboard this trip, downbound. Glad to hear you, Jim. Long time no hear! How are my sigs in Isle Royale?"

"S9 plus about 30 DB, Katchy. Sure sounds good to hear you again. How's the new ship? W8XI . . . this is W9ZZO with W9ZZY in the hole standing by for you. Go ahead."

"Roger, this is W8XI returning. The new ship's okay, so far! What's this I heard you telling Jerry about chasing moose? What's the big idea? You guys hard up for fresh meat out there on the rock? Take it, Jerry, over."

"I haven't got too much here. Gotta go eat, anyway, so

I'll turn it over to Jim. He can give you the dope on the moose. See you guys later. W9ZZY, Devil's Island signing off and clear."

"Okay, Jerry. S'long. See you tomorrow on schedule. Now, about the moose. Yup, guess we're going to see some fun. Don't know how they're going to do it, but it'll sure be worth watching. What kind of stuff did you say you had aboard, Katchy?"

"We've got grain in the hatches, Jim. Took on a big load at Duluth, downbound for Toledo. She's ridin' mighty low. Cap'n Jensen is praying for good weather, believe me, and so am I."

"How come?" Jim's fingers flipped the switches automatically back and forth from transmitter "on" to transmitter "off." It was necessary to identify the station every fifteen minutes while in QSO with another station. Sometimes, when more than two stations were in QSO, each station identified himself in turn, but with only two stations, this was not necessary.

"Well, Jim, this ship has seen better days. It's a good ship, don't get me wrong, but it needs plenty of work. They'll do it this winter when we tie up. Y'know, we've had some pretty big blows this season. Over."

"Guess you're right, at that. Lake Superior's kicked up her heels quite a bit. I know we've had to watch the weather pretty close, especially when we expect the supply boat. She'll take plenty of sea, but, just the same, there's no use taking chances. Where are you now?" Jim waited for an answer.

"Guess I'd better identify. This is W8XI/Marine Mobile, aboard the S. S. *Norcliff,* approximately fifty miles from Devil's Island, downbound. Say, Jim, how's the studying coming along? Still hitting the textbooks?"

"W8XI/Marine Mobile, this is W9ZZO, Isle Royale returning. Of course. I don't know whether I understand it all, but some of it's soaking in. Say, that Nilson Hornung book is a dandy. Gives all the answers. Got Ghirardi last spring, guess I told you that before. But between those two books and the *Radio Amateur's Handbook*, I've sure got myself a big case of mental indigestion." Jim's laugh was contagious and as he turned the transmitter plate switch off, he heard Katchy laughing, too.

"You're sure a 'bear for punishment,' kid . . . but luck to you, anyway. If there's anything I can do to help you, just holler. Woops! There goes the intercom. Cap'n wants me. See you later, Jim. Don't wait so long, next time. This is W8XI/Marine Mobile signing off and clear with W9ZZO. 'Bye, Jim."

"S'long, Katchy. See you later. This is W9ZZO, Isle Royale." Jim turned off the transmit switch and was about to turn off the filaments when he heard a faint call.

"Break! Break! W9ZZO, W9ZZO, break!"

Jim turned the receiver bandspread dial. The signal was weak but clear. He turned the gain open then turned on the transmit switch.

"Who's the breaker? This is W9ZZO, standing by for you."

"W9ZZO," the signal was swinging several degrees on the dial, "this is VE 3MZ/Mobile. Say, ol' man, I've been trying to raise someone closer but I'm almost out of gas, and I'm stuck here in a hole with a broken axle. Can you call some help for me from Port Arthur? Over."

"VE3MZ, this is W9ZZO. Sure. Where are you located? I'll find someone for you. Give me your location."

The signal was unsteady now. "I'm about seventy-five miles from Port Arthur, on the road to Saganaca Lake. We're almost in sight of the lake. . . . Do you copy?"

"Roger! Roger! VE3MZ, I'll get some help sent out to you somehow. Anybody hurt?"

The signal that Jim heard now was too weak to copy. He tuned carefully, volume wide open now, but it was no use. Evidently the mobile transmitter in VE3MZ's car had gone out.

Jim searched the band now, carefully, reading each signal with new interest. He must find a Canadian station who could either relay a message to Port Arthur or find a station in Port Arthur who could send help to the motorist in distress. He tuned to the frequency where he usually contacted one of the Canadian hams in Port Arthur, but several W9's occupied the frequency. Perhaps Jerry was still around. They could relay from Devil's Island.

"W9ZZY, W9ZZY, W9ZZY, this is W9ZZO, Isle Royale Calling. You around, Jerry?"

Jim tuned the receiver to 3924 kc. Jerry had evidently turned the receiver off. There was nothing on the frequency. Maybe he could raise a Canadian on a CQ. He could try.

"CQ Canada, CQ Canada, CQ Canada—urgent, CQ Canada, CQ Canada, CQ Canada. This is W9ZZO, Isle Royale calling any Canadian station with emergency traffic. W9ZZO standing by."

Only the crackle of static and several heterodynes from other ham stations came from the loudspeaker. Jim flipped the transmit switch again.

"9ZZO calling CQ Canada with urgent, emergency traffic. CQ Canada, CQ Canada, CQ Canada. Emergency traffic for Canada. CQ, CQ, CQ. This is Isle Royale, W9ZZO, calling and standing by. Come in, please!"

Still nothing was heard, except W's from the United States, and all busy in QSO. Twenty meters! Maybe he could work a Canadian on twenty. He turned the transmitter off.

His chair teetered precariously as he jumped up and began to pull coils from the inside of the transmitter. First the oscillator coil, then the buffer coil, the grid coil and finally the final plate coil and swinging link coil. Replacing each one in turn from the shelf of coils above the transmitter took but thirty seconds. Filaments on again, he tapped the desk impatiently with his fingers. Maybe the fellow was hurt, maybe there were others in the car, too! With a broken axle, the car might have gone in the ditch! All these thoughts jumbled about in his mind. There, now he could tune up. Long practice made it simple for Jim. He turned on the transmit switch, finally.

"CQ Canada, CQ Canada, CQ Canada with emergency traffic. CQ Canada, CQ Canada, CQ Canada." Tension built up in his voice as he silently prayed for someone to answer his CQ. "This is W9ZZO, Isle Royale calling CQ with emergency traffic and standing by."

The sound of a heterodyne slid across his frequency, then came back, steadied and held. Then—"W9ZZO, W9ZZO, W9ZZO—this is VE8IE. What's the matter, Jim, you sound frantic?"

"VE8IE, this is W9ZZO. Brother, am I gald to get you. I was down on seventy-five meters and got an emergency call from VE3MZ. He's mobile and stranded somewhere near Lake Saganaca with a broken axle. I don't know whether anyone's hurt or not but can you help us out, Torval?"

"Roger. Give me his approximate position, if you have it . . . and I'll contact the Mounties on the Police frequency. Over."

"He said he was about seventy-five miles from Port Arthur, on the old road to Saganaca Lake. That's about all I can tell you. Will that help?"

"You bet. I'll get on it right away. The Mounties have a Post about thirty miles east of where he is, so don't worry. And say, Jim, thanks a million. I'm glad you got that much before his signals quit. See you later. We'll have another game of checkers one of these days. VE8IE off and clear."

Jim breathed a long sigh of relief as he pushed back his chair and stretched his long legs under the desk. He pictured the car, in a ditch with a broken axle, and maybe someone hurt. He also pictured a man sitting helplessly behind the wheel, microphone in hand, with either a dead battery or no gas. He wondered how he'd feel under the same circumstances.

"Jim!" The sound of Chuck's voice brought him back to reality. He could see his brother standing on the porch of the cabin, with Hill Billy chattering noisily on his shoulder. "Jim-m-m-m . . ."

"Be right with you, Chuck . . ." Jim scribbled hastily in the log book for a moment before he hurried out and shut the door.

Jim had left oatmeal and hot chocolate on the back of the stove to keep warm until he came in. He dished out big bowlsful for both boys and took them into their bedroom on a tray, his mind still on the Canadian in distress.

"How's the head, kid?" he asked as he plumped the pillows behind Jack's back so he could sit up to eat.

"Better, Jim." Jack sniffed the appetizing steam as it circled over the tray. "Come on, Chuck, you can eat with me—huh, Jim?"

"Sure thing. It's all there. If you want anything more —holler!"

A few minutes later, when Chuck plunked the empty tray down on the kitchen table, Jim said, "I'll do the dishes, if you'll stay home with Jack while I take a run down to the school. How about it?"

"Sure." Chuck agreed, glad to do anything that would save him from dishes. "I'm going to put up my new house anyway, and—" he wrinkled up his pug nose—"who wants to go to school, anyhow?"

"I won't be gone long. Be sure to stay near the house, so if Jack wants anything, you'll hear him call."

"Okay?" Jim turned to look at Jack. The bandage on the injured boy's head had turned dark now—but the bleeding had stopped.

"Okay, but I think I'll stay in bed."

"I'll say you're going to stay in bed—high diver!" Jim said emphatically. "Is there anything you want? Maybe I'd better change that bandage."

"Naw—it's okay."

"I won't hurt you—"

"I know it," Jack answered listlessly. "Go ahead and change it then."

While he changed the bandage, Jim talked about everything he could think of that might interest Jack. He observed, with satisfaction, that the jagged wound had stopped bleeding and was beginning to form a thin scab. If they didn't disturb it for a day or so, it would heal nicely.

Jack waited until Jim had finished before he spoke. "I heard you tell Chuck you were going to school. If you see any of the other kids, Bill or any of the others, tell 'em I'll be seeing them—"

"I'll tell them if I see them and I won't be gone long. Think you'll be all right till I get back?" Jim hesitated. "I won't go if—"

"Heck, I'll be okay. I can finish some of my boat. Sure, go ahead! Don't forget to tell Bill what I told you, if you see him."

"I won't."

After giving Jack his carving set and his birch knot, Jim hurried out. Chuck sat on the porch with Hill Billy, his new squirrel house on his lap. He seemed to be in no hurry to hang it up. Jim warned him again to stay near Jack.

The walk to the school took Jim about fifteen minutes, during which time his thoughts were racing from the conversation earlier with his friends on seventy-five meters to his ever present problem.

As he neared the clearing, he could see the small schoolhouse nestled sedately in a semi-circle of fir trees, its green shutters contrasting with its weather-beaten walls. Smoke rolled from the chimney.

Jim wondered just why he'd come down to the school. Curiosity, he explained to himself—and perhaps for a sympathetic listener. He wanted to talk to someone about going to summer school. Maybe he could mention it casually to the new teacher. Then again, maybe he'd better keep still. He hesitated on the bottom step and was about to turn around and go back home when he stopped short. Someone was singing! He tiptoed up the rest of the steps and opened the door, then stood and stared. Wow! The new teacher was dancing all by herself—and could she dance! Jim stared some more.

In the middle of a twirl, the young lady saw the boy standing in the doorway and stopped short, a smile of amusement and embarrassment on her flushed face. "Oh, I didn't know I had an audience!" she gasped. Her black eyes sparkled and her mouth seemed to hold laughter in its corners. Jim had never seen such golden hair matched with black eyes.

He blushed, then stammered, "I—I'm sorry, er— I'm Jim St. Cyr."

"I'm glad you dropped in, Jim. I'm Gene Gregory, the new teacher. I was wondering if any of my pupils would stop around to see me today." She pushed a loosened ringlet back from her forehead. "I'd almost given up hope."

Jim fidgeted in the doorway. "I was just out for a walk and saw smoke coming from the chimney and thought I'd drop in for a minute. I can't stay. My brother got hurt yesterday and I told him I wouldn't be long."

"Come in a moment anyway, won't you?" Miss Gregory said. "I was through with all my work. How old is your brother?" She sat down and started to stack the papers on her desk and Jim knew it would be impolite to back out now. Besides, his father was right! She was "Quite a dish." He walked over to the desk he used during the winter months, and sat down, too.

"It won't be long before we'll be back at the old grind

again!" he observed. Then, when he saw Miss Gregory turn her head to conceal a smile, he added quickly, "I mean —er— Golly! I meant it won't be long before school starts again." This time, the blush that rose to the edge of his hair practically matched it in color.

"Yes," Miss Gregory grinned at him, "it won't be long now!" Then they both laughed. After that, they chatted easily together and Jim gave her a few interesting side-lights on the rest of the families whose children she'd be teaching.

"Tell me about my pupils, Jim—" she urged.

"There're the Johnson kids, from down the island—four of 'em. Bill's Jack's chum."

"Oh. Is his father a Ranger, too?"

"Heck-no!" Jim laughed. "Ole Johnson's a fisherman. They've only been here about two years. He sells his white fish and lake trout to the weekly steamer."

"*Hum*— Who else, Jim?"

"Oh, there're the Butlers. They've got two girls. And Mickey Reed. His dad's a fisherman, too."

"It looks as if I'll be busy, all right." She asked, then, "What about our mail?"

"Gee—didn't they tell you? Mail planes drop us our mail in the winter."

"I guess they did mention it, but I'd forgotten. I certainly hope nobody gets sick. How would we get him off the island?"

"In winter they only land in case of an emergency."

"Oh!" She glanced at her watch.

Jim jumped to his feet. "Howling cats! I've got to be getting home. I said I wouldn't stay and here I've been chewing the fat, er—I mean talking—for half an hour! My kid brothers will be wondering what happened to me. And I've missed a schedule with the mainland."

"Is that serious?"

"Serious? Golly, Miss Gregory, you sure have a lot to learn!" He turned at the door. "I don't suppose you'd care to come home with me for lunch, we call it dinner on the island, would you? The kids'd like to see you!" He knew she'd make a definite hit with the two younger St. Cyrs.

Miss Gregory hesitated a moment before answering. "Are you sure that I wouldn't be intruding, Jim?"

"Of course not. And maybe you could look at Jack— see if he's really okay. Of course—I'm sure he is—but—"

"I'd love to go."

Jim's face was stretched from ear to ear with a great big grin. "We'll have to hurry."

He closed and locked the schoolhouse door for her and led the way down the path toward the cabin. Suddenly, he turned and looked at her over his shoulder. "It's about a fifteen-minute hike," he said.

"Lead on MacDuff!" She laughed. "You don't scare me a bit."

As they reached the last ridge, minutes later, Miss Gregory stopped abruptly. "What a beautiful picture that makes!" she exclaimed. The cabin in the clearing, its bright red roof nestled like a ruby in a bed of green cotton, appeared almost like an artificial stage setting.

"I suppose it is," Jim answered without much enthusiasm. Then he saw Chuck racing toward them. "We've been sighted. Here comes my youngest brother—he's six."

"He's in a big hurry. Gracious, what's that on his shoulder?" Miss Gregory asked.

"Oh, that's just Hill Billy, his pet squirrel." Jim laughed. "Chuckie has other pets, but this squirrel is his favorite. Goes everywhere with him. The others—well, we never see them, but he tells us about them," he explained as Chuck stopped in front of them. "Chuck, this is Miss Gregory, our new teacher."

Chuck stuck out a slightly grimy hand and said, " 'Lo."

"Hello, Charles," Miss Gregory murmured. "What a cute pet you have. May I hold him or is he afraid of strangers?" She held out her hand but Hill Billy ran up and sat on Chuck's head, scolding furiously.

Chuck grinned. "You see, he has to get used to you before he'll let you take him. Down, Hill Billy!" he scolded. "The lady won't hurt you."

Hill Billy's beady black eyes took in the situation sharply. He evidently decided there was no danger, for he ran down to perch on Chuckie's shoulder again as they all walked to the cabin.

Miss Gregory glanced around as they entered, and her black eyebrows lifted in wonder.

"What a lovely home you boys have! Don't tell me that you do all the work here. I can hardly believe it!"

"Oh, it isn't hard work, when we all pitch in," Jim answered. "Jack does most of the cooking, because he likes it. Chuckie dusts and keeps things straightened up and picked up, and I do the scrubbing." He laughed. "Of course, we aren't experts but we manage. Dad does anything and everything, but we try to have it done before he gets home. He's a Forest Ranger, you know."

"Jim, is that you?" Jack's voice called from the bedroom. "I thought you'd never come home. Is the new teacher pretty like Dad said? Is she young?" Jim looked at Miss Gregory, aghast, then hurried into the bedroom.

Chuck smiled up at Miss Gregory and filled in the awkward pause. "Want to come in the front room? There's a fire in the fireplace—" He took her by the hand and led her to a big easy chair in front of the hearth, then said abruptly, "Scuse me!" and followed his big brother into the bedroom.

A moment later, Jim came into the living room. "Jack's anxious to see you," he suggested. "Would you mind?"

"I've been wondering where you disappeared to. I'd like to meet him."

It took but a moment for the two to get acquainted and, after a few leading questions from Miss Gregory, Jack was telling her all about his accident. Jim excused himself and went out to the kitchen to start lunch.

In a few minutes Jim interrupted the accident saga with Jack's tray and discovered that the teacher was already "Miss Gene" to his brothers.

"Lunch is ready. We don't have to wait for Dad. He should be here any minute, though." Jim escorted the new teacher to the kitchen table and pulled out her chair. "This isn't very fancy, Miss Gregory, but it's good."

"That hike down here gave me a terrific appetite, Jim. This looks like a feast!"

They had just started to eat when steps sounded on the screened porch and Mr. St. Cyr opened the door. "I guess I'm just in time—well, Miss Gregory, I see the boys have corraled you already. This is great! How do you like Isle Royale so far?"

"I think it's the most fascinating place I've ever seen.

Of course, I haven't seen much of it yet, but what I've experienced so far has been lovely. And these boys of yours, they can do so many things!" She laughed. "All the boys I've known have seemed so helpless and not able even to dress themselves properly. You certainly should be proud of your sons!"

The Ranger's warm smile spread to his eyes. "Yes, I'm very proud of them, Miss Gregory. I think they're all mighty capable. I've had to leave them on their own much of the time and I don't remember of any instance where they haven't done everything they were told to do —and sometimes things that they weren't told to do," he added with a meaningful wink.

"Sit down, Dad," Jim broke in hastily, with an embarrassed grin, "and no more of that blarney for today." Why did older people always discuss children right in front of them, like so many cows—or horses!

It was two o'clock before any of the group noticed the time.

Jim excused himself. "I've got to report to the mainland. Anything you want me to tell 'em, Dad?"

"No, I guess not. I'll talk to them later."

When Jim re-entered the kitchen a while later, his father was getting ready to accompany Miss Gene back to school.

"I think I'll walk along with you, Dad," Jim remarked and pulled on his heavy mackinaw. He didn't add the thought that was in his mind, but he intended to speak to his father about radio summer school at Michigan Tech. He didn't want to stay on the island next summer, after he'd graduated. He must speak to his father and make him see that he just wasn't suited for Ranger life. He really only existed when he was tinkering at his radio bench or building up a new radio set out of bits of odds and ends, or talking to his many friends over his short wave station.

Miss Gene said good-bye to Jack and Chuck and tried to make friends with Hill Billy before she left, but the squirrel was busy digging in Chuck's pocket for nuts.

As they walked up the trail, the Ranger began, "I want to tell you how much I appreciate your coming over for lunch with the boys—" But she stopped this with a wave of her hand.

"But I have enjoyed it, Mr. St. Cyr."

He replied, "You must come often. We were glad to have you."

In front of the school house, Miss Gregory stopped and held out her hand to Mr. St. Cyr. "Thanks again for the lovely lunch and for the pleasure of being with your family." To Jim, she said, "It was sweet of you to invite me over, good-bye." And turning, she ran up the steps.

"Golly, Dad!" Jim exclaimed, "I never knew there were teachers like her. I think I'm going to like school this year!"

Retracing their steps up the trail, with the Ranger in the lead, there was little opportunity for conversation and Jim had no chance to open the subject of summer school until they neared the porch of their cabin.

"Oh, Dad, I talked to Tom this morning, and he's going to Michigan Tech next summer—"

Jim looked at his father out of the corners of his eyes.

"And, Dad, I'd like to go, too!" After he had spoken the words, Jim wished he hadn't. Roger's lips straightened and he stopped and turned.

"I don't want to hear any more nonsense about summer school. You know I need you in the summer and besides," he cleared his throat, "you're too young to go gallivanting off to school alone!"

"After all, I'm seventeen!" Jim stretched up to his full six feet. "I'm not a baby any more."

"But who'll look after the boys? They're too young to leave alone while I'm away!"

Jim had no answer.

Mr. St. Cyr walked into the house and Jim leaned against the porch railing. The pleasant day was soured again and he snorted with disgust as he walked to the radio shack.

Nursemaid! Ranger! Howling cats! Couldn't a guy even make up his own mind about what he wanted to do? He didn't want to hurt his father and yet, he just had to find a way to get to radio school next summer.

Why couldn't his dad understand? Fathers were supposed to want what was best for their children. Why was he having such a hard time trying to make him understand?

Jim stood at the door of the ham shack for a moment and looked out across Lake Superior. The sun was almost gone. Rays of deep scarlet, gold, thousands of in-between shades cast their fading glow into the heavens. The tinge of frost, pine, leaves settling into a thick mat on the forest floor around him reminded the young man that fall was at hand.

Ever since he could remember, his father, in more serious moments, had told the boys, "No matter what you want, if you want it badly enough, work hard enough, pray hard enough, some day your wish will come true."

Jim grunted. He couldn't be doing something right, wishing or working or praying, he mused. Maybe that was the answer. But how could that change his father's mind? No, there must be some other answer. He pushed open the door and lit one of the Aladdin lamps. It would be swell, he thought, when they got the new generator to supply electric power. It had been ordered weeks ago. He wondered, briefly, why it hadn't come.

He looked at his watch. It was too late to contact the fellows on twenty meters. There was just a chance that Jerry might be around yet on 75.

As he changed the transmitter coils back to 75 meters, impatience with his father disappeared. In its place was a question. What was the reason? Why couldn't he swing his father to his viewpoint?

Soon the transmitter was warmed up and ready to take Jim away from the island. Questions were still buzzing around in his thoughts as he carefully tuned the 75 meter phone band. A loud signal was coming through on 3900. He listened for a moment. Yes, it was Katchy, talking with someone in Detroit. Jim tuned the transmitter VFO to the same frequency, then waited for a chance to break them.

"Break, break!" He flipped switches fast.

"Someone's trying to break us," the Detroit station said. "Breaker, come in."

"This is W9ZZO, Isle Royale. How's chances to join the QSO? Heard Katchy yacking away there. Both signals are S9 plus up here on the island. Over."

"Roger. W9ZZO, W8XI/Marine mobile, this is W8MAZ, Detroit, right back. Good to hear you, Jim. How's everything on the island? S'pose you're getting ready for the winter about now, huh? How many traps you going to put out this year? Katchy's havin' trouble. How about it, Katchy? W8XI/Marine Mobile to take it, with W9ZZO and W8MAZ standing by."

"W9ZZO, W8MAZ, W8XI/Marine Mobile. Roger. Hi, Jim. Nice signal down here. We're upbound with some coal for Ashland this trip. Having some trouble with the commercial transmitter. Got some replacements in Toledo and have a little more work to do on it yet. Hey— what goes with that rescue job I heard about today from Jerry?"

"W9ZZO. What did you hear? I couldn't get anyone on 75 so I went to 20 meters and got Torval. I'm anxious to hear what happened. But first, back to Detroit. What's the handle down there? W8XI/Marine Mobile, to W8MAZ, this is W9ZZO standing by."

"W8MAZ returning. Roger on both transmissions. Handle here's Tear Easy Xray—Tex. Sure glad to hook up with you, ol' man. What's all this about a rescue job? I'll turn it back to Katchy. I'm all ears!"

"Okay, Tex. Well, Jim, I talked to Jerry on Devil's Island and he'd just come down from twenty meters, too. He'd been in QSO with a Canadian who wanted him to contact a Canadian in Port Arthur. Of course, Torval, up there in No Man's Land had talked to this guy in Port Arthur and also to Jerry and he arranged the sked. So the ham in Port Arthur and Jerry shifted to 75 and got the Mounties on this mobile's trail. Kind of a roundabout mess, but it did the trick. The Mounties got on it right away and found the mobile. It seems that there were three fellows going fishing up at Saganaca. I didn't get all the details but only one of them was hurt. I think he was thrown over the front seat when the car hit the hole and his leg got bent the wrong way over some camping gear they had on the floor of the back seat. They're all back at Port Arthur now, though, thanks to you, Jim. Over."

"Right. Well, I'm glad I heard the guy before his mobile quit on him. It's a lucky thing they didn't have to hoof it all the way back to Port Arthur, carrying that injured man. Not much more here, fellows. See you later. Nice meeting you, Tex. Give me a call whenever you hear me. W8XI Marine Mobile, to W8MAZ, Detroit, this is W9ZZO, Isle Royale, signing off and clear and pulling the big switch. S'long."

Jim leaned back in the chair. Time for supper. Maybe he could persuade his dad tonight. Too bad Jack had to get banged up, but he'd be all right in a day or two.

The tall redhead rose, turned off the Aladdin lamp, closed the door quietly and walked slowly to the cabin.

5

vvvv • vvvv • vvvv • vvvv • vvvv • vvvv • vvvv

Sunday was the one day of the week when all the St. Cyrs could sleep late. Mr. St. Cyr had only to make out his weekly report on the movements of the moose herd and the condition of the forests, and radio it to the mainland.

Often the family gathered in the ham shack while Jim chatted with other hams in other hams shacks around the world.

Today, Jim headed for the shack right after a late breakfast. Today, he could call his own. His father would be home all day, and would get the meals, as well as watch Chuck.

A little fire, to warm the ham shack, and Jim could talk as long as he wanted to without having any Ranger responsibilities on his mind. He turned on the filaments of both the receiver and transmitter before he started the fire in the buck stove. As the receiver warmed up, he could hear Jerry on Devil's Island talking with Katchy.

With the fire blazing mightily at his back, Jim settled
before his desk for a long, leisurely chat with his friends.
He tuned the VFO to their frequency and tuned the final
of the transmitter for maximum output.

"Break! Break!" He got it in before Katchy could come
back to Jerry with his next transmission.

"Sounds like our friend on the island wants in. You
think we should talk to him, Jerry?"

"Waaal, seein's as how it's Jim, and Jim is all set for a
long-winded session, this being Sunday an' all, yeah—I
guess we might as well talk to him. Come on in, Jim, the
QRM's just dandy."

The two hams liked to razz Jim because he was always
good-natured.

"W8XI/Marine Mobile, W9ZZY, this is W9ZZO, Isle
Royale. Hey, you two windbags better get a new line.
That one's about fit to bury. What's going on today?
Anything of interest?"

"W8XI/Marine Mobile returning. Oh, I guess everything is under control. Storm warnings are up, though.
Been up all morning. How about it, Jerry? What's the
latest weather report? W9ZZY to take it, W8XI and
W9ZZO in the hole."

"Roger. Let's see, the latest weather. Still brewing up
a storm, Katchy. I'm glad I'm not out on ol' Superior today. She's really cookin' up a dandy. I forgot to ask you
where you are, Katchy. Break back and give us your location. Over."

"We're on Lake Michigan, northbound through the
Straits of Mackinaw to the Soo Locks. Over."

"Right. Well, Jim, sure glad it's Sunday. All the hams
in the country are on today by the sound of it. But you're

about the loudest signal on the band right now. What's on your mind?"

"W8XI, W9ZZY, this is W9ZZO. 75 sure sounds crowded. Say, Katchy, what time you going through the locks?"

"We're through the Straits now, going into Lake Huron. In fact, in about fifteen minutes we'll be in St. Mary's River. And say, it's getting pretty rocky out here. Of course, it won't be bad when we hit the river but I sure hope it lets up by the time we get through the locks. I don't like the looks of those thunderheads north of us. Maybe it'll be over by the time we hit Whitefish Bay. Take it, Jerry. I'm going to get a cup of mud. Be right back."

"Righto! Say, Jim, stand by a minute. There's something coming in on the distress frequency. It's an SOS! Hold it!"

Jim, seated before his desk on the island, could hear and read the code coming through the commercial receiver on Devil's Island. Jerry, obviously, hadn't switched off the transmitter. Jim listened carefully. Was it really an emergency message? He copied the last part of the message down. It read: "—off the coast of Isle Royale. Can you send help?"

Tense now, Jim waited for Jerry's reply. It came, sharp and clear, for Jerry used a bug and he could send perfect code. Jim read aloud as he copied, "Will contact Isle Royale and Coast Guard. How long will you float?"

The answer came. "Come quickly. We've sprung a bulkhead. Don't know how long we can stay afloat. Pumps can't handle it much longer. All hands bailing. Over."

"Hang tough! Stay on frequency. Stand by!" Jim heard a rustle of papers and heard a shout from his father at the same time that Jerry called him from Devil's Island.

"Jim, there's a pleasure yacht, the *Leonora* in bad trouble off Rock of Ages Light. Do you have a boat there?"

"Jim!" The Ranger was running down the path to the ham shack now. "Jim!" He burst through the doorway. "Cut out that chatter! We've more important work to do. There's a boat in distress off Rock of Ages. Come on!"

Jim had switched the transmitter on so Jerry must have heard his father. Jim finished with, "Sorry, Jerry. Dad didn't know I was talking to you. Yes, we have the Ranger boat here, we'll see what we can do—won't we, Dad?" He turned to his father with the question.

Mr. St. Cyr obviously felt ashamed. "Yes," he replied. "I was listening on 51. The Coast Guard is sending out a crash boat and asked if we could help them. They're not sure they can reach them in time, if the yacht is badly damaged. We can keep in touch with the transceiver."

"We'll see you in a few minutes then, Jerry. Watch for me on 51. Over."

"Okay! I'll see you in about ten minutes. I've got to clear the crash boat. Pretty rough going for that small a boat but a lifeboat would never reach them in time. Luck! 9ZZY clear."

"W9ZZO clear." Jim glanced at the clock. 11:55 a.m. He could fill in the log later.

With one sweeping motion, (so it seemed to Mr. St. Cyr) Jim turned off the transmitter, receiver, VFO and lights and followed his father to the cabin on the run. Gathering up warm clothes, slickers, the portable transceiver, they paused long enough to tell Jack to stand by the transmitter on emergency 51, just in case he'd be needed to relay any message. Although the boy had no license, he had learned to operate the Ranger transmitter by watching his father and older brother.

At the pier, Ranger St. Cyr checked the gas gauge on their boat, to make sure it registered full. Jim put the transceiver in the small cabin and came back out to help his father.

Waves were pounding high as they pulled away from shore and both looked back at their home. They could see Chuck standing on the porch, waving, trying to catch their attention. They waved back at him.

There was a frown on Mr. St. Cyr's face as he headed their sturdy boat out into open water. White caps curled foamy fingers up into the air, then tipped them under. He didn't like this at all, especially since Jim was with him. There was no room on Lake Superior for both a storm and small craft at the same time.

Water sprayed over the sides of the boat every time they nosed into a wave crest. Rivers of water ran from their slickers into the sloshing water on deck, as it raced madly fore and aft each time the boat hit a wave, then quivered high for an instant before it plunged, nose down, on the other side.

There was speed in the inboard motor but today it seemed to be standing still. Helmsman St. Cyr stayed as close to the shoreline as he could, without hitting the shallows. He knew his coastline without consulting charts. If the calculations were right, the yacht must be somewhere this side of Rock of Ages Light. It would take at least an hour to make it. By then, if the ship was really in bad trouble, it might be too late.

Jim yelled into his father's ear. "Hadn't I better contact them, if I can?"

"Yes," Roger St. Cyr nodded in agreement. "Find out where the Coast Guard crash boat is, too. They'd better make it before we do. At this rate, we'll never get there!"

Jim disappeared into the cabin again and came out a moment later with the transceiver. Small, compact, a handy thing for a Ranger to carry, the 10-watt transceiver put out a signal that could be read by Jerry, on Devil's Island, under good weather conditions.

Jim pulled the antenna out and extended the metal rod as far as it would go. This turned on the small transmitter and receiver. In a moment it was ready. He spoke into the microphone.

"W9ZZO calling anyone on this frequency who can hear me. W9ZZO standing by."

The Ranger turned to his son. "You were using your ham call, did you realize it?"

"I did?" Jim, keyed to a high pitch of excitement, was obviously unaware of anything except the seriousness of the situation and the danger they were facing with every plunge of the small boat.

Earphones clamped against his ears, he listened intently. He stood braced against the cabin door, feet apart for leverage. Anxiously, he called again.

"W9ZZO calling Crash Boat. ZZO to Crash Boat. Do you copy?"

No answer came; nothing but the roar from the motor sounded through the earphones.

"Calling Crash Boat, calling Crash Boat, this is Ranger

boat with W9ZZO at the mike calling you. Do you copy?"

Still no answer broke through the noise.

The waves were breaking high over the prow now, drenching everything with heavy spray. The water was a deep, dark green, deadly, treacherous. The smell of oil mixed with the unmistakable odor of churning, weed filled, fresh water filled the air.

Jim tried again. "W9ZZO calling Coast Guard Crash Boat, come in Crash Boat!" He pressed the earphone to his head with his free hand. The expression on his face changed suddenly.

He waved his free hand at his father. "They heard us! They did hear us!" He pressed the microphone switch to transmit.

"Roger! Roger! I copy you. We are on our way. How far are you from Rock of Ages?"

The Ranger was too busy keeping the nose of the boat pointed head on, into the high waves, to hear what his son was saying.

Jim was talking again. "You've sighted the boat? It's still afloat? Over."

His eyes were shut tightly as he concentrated on the answer. There was QRN from the brushes on the inboard motor and only by concentration could he hear the Coast Guard crash boat's answer.

"Yes. I'll tell him. We are okay." Jim opened his eyes now, as if to seek confirmation from his father but the latter was still too concerned with holding the wheel steady to pay much attention to anything else.

"Dad!"

Mr. St. Cyr turned his head slightly then to include Jim in his vision. "Yes?"

"The Coast Guard crash boat crew has sighted them and says they're still afloat. They said they didn't need us and thanks!"

The Ranger yelled his answer into the wind. "They must have been pretty close."

"They were coming down from Pigeon Bay and were only about fifteen minutes from the Rock, so it didn't take them too long to find the yacht. That's what I call dumb luck."

His father just nodded. He was having trouble turning around. He watched intently for a good chance. The rollers were high. He'd have to make a quick turn or be swamped by the back lash of a wave. For a few minutes it seemed as though there'd never be a break. Jim kept the earphones tight to his ears, his eyes shut. His face was white. He'd never been out on Superior when it was this rough; he'd only listened to frightening tales of fishermen lost in storms on the Lake. Lost, and their bodies never found! He'd heard the legend about Superior never giving up her dead. He'd heard it many times. The boat gave a sudden lurch and Jim fell forward to his knees. When he regained his feet, they were headed for home.

He looked at his father. The Ranger gave him a tight-lipped smile, but he still fought the wheel at every wave crest.

Jim yelled at him, "They're just taking the passengers off the boat now. The pumps are still operating, and they're going to try to tow her in."

"If she sinks, she'll pull them all down!"

"They're watching it," Jim called. "I heard them tell Jerry they'd cut her loose if they have to. But they'll try to get her in first."

"Good old Coast Guard!"

Jim disappeared into the cabin and came out a moment later without the transceiver.

"Need any help?" he asked, his voice almost a shout to be heard above the roar of the pounding waves and wind.

The Ranger shook his head, no, and Jim stayed where he was, braced against the cabin.

He relaxed just a little now. They were headed for home. With the tension which had built up within him gone, he reviewed the past hour. A near-tragedy had been averted and, although they had tried to be of help, he was glad the Coast Guard boat had reached the yacht first. Powerful and speedy, although not as seaworthy as a Coast Guard thirty-six foot lifeboat, the thirty foot crash boat had taken a dangerous chance in this high sea.

A few minutes later, when Jim and his father finally sighted the pier in front of the cabin, they could see both Jack and Chuck waiting for them—Jack with the Ranger glasses, watching intently, and Chuck with Hill Billy.

Shaken and pale, both Mr. St. Cyr and Jim were glad to reach shore.

As they secured the Ranger boat, they answered the questions that tumbled from the two boys as best they could.

"Did somebody drown?" Chuck asked breathlessly, first.

"No," his father tousled the youngster's hair, "of course not! What a morbid question!"

"Morbid? What's that?"

They all laughed. "I mean, where did you get that terrible idea?"

"Golly!" Chuck was hanging on to his father's hand

now as they all walked back to the cabin. "The way you and Jim ran when you left us, I thought somebody sunk!"

"Nope! Nobody sunk!" Mr. St. Cyr chuckled, then asked Jim over his shoulder, "Bring the transceiver?"

"Yup." Jim patted it as it dangled from his shoulder. "I'm going to the shack. See how they're making out."

"Okay."

Mr. St. Cyr, Jack and Chuck continued on to the cabin while Jim cut across to the ham shack. He was anxious to get back on the air. There was no motor noise to interfere with the receiver now, so he could easily find out what had happened.

He threw another large chunk of wood in the stove, stirred it a little and then settled down at his desk. With the transmitter and receiver again ready, he spoke into the mike.

"W9ZZO calling W9ZZY. You around, Jerry?"

"W9ZZO, this is W9ZZY. Yeah. Been waiting for you. Knew you'd be back on. Say, that was kind of a wild ride you guys had, eh? Over."

"Kind of's not the word for it!" Jim answered emphatically. "I'm sure glad to be back on dry land. What happened?"

"Well," Jerry on Devil's Island explained, "the Coast Guard found them wallowing around in the trough, about a quarter mile off Rock of Ages. Another few minutes and they'd have either smashed up on the rocks or gone down. The skipper of the yacht had been warned, but he was too bullheaded to pay any attention to the storm warnings and went out, anyway. He hit a submerged rock somewhere—he was a bit vague as to where—and opened up a seam. They were taking in plenty of water and the pumps could just about handle it and that's all. He panicked. But everything's under control and the crash boat has them in tow. They're making for Pigeon Bay, Canada. It's calmer there. W9ZZO, this is W9ZZY standing by."

"Fine, Jerry. I'm sure glad it turned out okay. Brother, that wind sure was kicking up a fuss out there! Say, how did the portable sound?"

"Sounded good, but only about Q2 R4. Knew it was you and had the gain on the receiver wide open to read you. Good thing you were on 51. I'd never have heard you on 75 meters in this QRM. Well, guess I can't do any more damage here and have lots of work to catch up on. See you later, Jim. Take 'er easy. W9ZZY off and clear with W9ZZO, Isle Royale, and W9ZZY pulling the big switch. S'long."

"S'long, Jerry. W9ZZO clear." Jim relaxed at last. It had been a wild day, certainly not one they would have picked for a ride on Lake Superior. He turned off the receiver. Better get the shack straightened up a little before he did any more hamming or he'd never get it done. Twenty meters should be good tonight, he thought, as he grabbed the broom and began to sweep wires, solder and sand into a little pile.

His energetic spurt of cleaning gave him time to review the day's experience. He knew now how lucky he and his father had been to reach home safely. A small boat in the high seas on Superior today was in constant danger. Their rescue expedition could have ended tragically. He said a small, but fervent prayer. "Thanks, God."

It was almost seven-thirty before Jim put the broom away. He was in no mood now for any more hamming.

He walked slowly to the cabin.

When he went inside, he found his father, who was smoking his pipe by the fireplace, relaxed, the tension of the afternoon gone now. He asked, "Did you take that piece of ham we've been using from the root cellar this morning?"

"Of course not! What'd I be doing with a chunk of ham? Why?" There was no place to keep a piece of ham that large except in the root cellar.

"As I was leaving the shack, I noticed the door of the cellar was open and thought maybe one of you was inside. I went over but there was no one there." Jim looked puzzled. "I looked around and noticed the ham was gone. Sure you didn't take it?"

"Sure!" Mr. St. Cyr exploded, "Of course I'm sure. Did you shut the door again?"

Jim nodded emphatically. "Maybe we'd better go out and look around," he added.

"I think so, too," his father agreed, and Chuck chimed in with his, "Can I go, too?"

When Mr. St. Cyr said he could, Chuck grabbed his hat and, with coat flying from one arm, ran out ahead of the other two.

Jim could see Hill Billy clinging to the collar of Chuck's sweater, bracing himself with his long, bushy tail to keep from being tossed into space.

Jim walked ahead, pushed open the door of the root cellar and flashed his big light around the inside.

A long frame had been built along the left wall. Huge sides of pork and beef dangled from the top of the rack. Four smoked hams hung from hooks. At the far end of the cellar stood the various bins for potatoes, turnips, onions and apples.

Cabbages, with the outer layers a dry tan color, were tied to a rope line, stretched high above the bins. A keg of sand held the winter supply of carrots, buried deep to keep them fresh and crisp. Lettuce heads, each wrapped carefully in waxed paper, rested on a high shelf next to the damp earth walls. The entire right side of the spacious root cellar was lined with wooden shelves, built on a movable frame.

The shelves were loaded with canned fruit and vegetables of various kinds, some home-canned and others in tin. Another tier held home-canned venison, rabbit and partridge.

In the center of the cellar stood a butcher's block. Its impressive row of knives and cleavers for cleaning and cutting meat and wild game shone weirdly in the sharp glow of the flashlight.

Jim pointed to the empty hook, on which the shank end of a bulky ham had hung. The sand on the carrot keg had been disturbed, as if some careless or hurried hand had explored, found what it sought, then its owner had rushed away.

One of the sharp knives was gone from the perfect row, leaving a hole like an extracted tooth.

"Well, I'll be—" The Ranger turned from the empty hook to the row of knives. "Someone is either trying to play a joke on us, or it is no joke!"

"Who do you suppose would do a thing like that?" Jim asked.

"Maybe it's Injun spooks!" Chuckie whispered loudly.

"Nonsense! As long as I've been here, nothing like this has ever happened. The people on the island are all honest, and besides, they have plenty of food in their own cellars. Someone must be hungry, but he could ask for something to eat—" Mr. St. Cyrs' face was flushed with annoyance. "We have never turned anyone away empty-handed yet. This is going a little too far."

Jim said, "We'd better lock the door with a good strong lock tonight!"

"I'll tend to that," Roger St. Cyr's voice had a determined ring as he closed the door and followed his sons back into the house.

While Jim was helping Jack undress and get ready for bed, he heard his father go out. Obviously, he was going to fix up the lock so that no one could break in again. When both Jack and Chuck were tucked in for the night, Jim stirred the embers in the fireplace and put another log on, then went out into the kitchen. He was raiding the icebox when his father returned.

"It'll take a pickax to get in there now without a key," he growled. "Of all the nerve!"

Hours later, Jim moved uneasily in his sleep. Suddenly he sat up in bed, eyes wide open, trying to pierce the dark.

"Wonder what woke me up?" he mumbled sleepily, rubbing his eyes and shaking his head, "There it is again!" As he spoke, another dull thud broke the stillness.

He reached for his flashlight and switched it on, carefully shading it with his hand.

Slipping his feet into the fur-lined muck-lucks at the edge of his bed, he tiptoed softly across the bedroom to the door of the kitchen.

A dull red circle flickered on the ceiling as the coal fire in the kitchen range shot its blood-red rays up around the edges of the lids.

Quietly, Jim crept to the back door. Again that dull thud! He turned off his light and slowly opened the outside door. It made no noise as he swung it back far enough to slip his long frame through. The sound outside was much louder now and his eyes turned to the root cellar, standing darkly visible there in the moonlight.

As he peered sharply into the deep night, his vision cleared and he could see a shadow by the door of the cellar. Then the shadow moved. Jim shivered, more from tension than from the cold, and he asked himself, almost aloud, "Who the dickens would prowl around here at night?"

He inched to the edge of the porch, still concealed by the heavy shadows, and put an exploring foot on the second step. The first step always squeaked and he remembered just in time to skip it. He eased himself down from there to the bottom step, then to solid earth. Cautiously, he moved to the edge of the cabin. The intruder, whoever he was, had not seen him yet. The dark brown of his bathrobe blended with the night darkness.

Gathering himself for one last lunge, he raced from the corner of the cabin to the cellar. Whoever stood at the door of the root cellar was not aware of his presence until he was almost upon him, then the trespasser wheeled with a sharp cry just as Jim turned on his light.

Instead of the thieving scoundrel Jim had expected, he saw the lanky, ragged figure of a young boy, about Jack's age, standing in the sharp circle of the flashlight's glow. His clothes were dirty and torn, his shoes had long since lost all shape and form. His hair hung almost to his shoulders. It was tangled into a thick mat of curls and snarls, which he had pushed back and hooked around his ears.

He crumpled to the ground, looking like a pile of old rags. The rock with which he had been pounding the lock rolled from his hand.

"Gosh! Who are you? What do you want?" Jim cried out, the excitement loosening his tongue with inane questions.

The boy began to cry with long sobbing wails, as if a hard struggle had suddenly come to an end and something tight inside had eased. A torrent of tears coursed down the pinched face.

Jim knelt quickly and put an arm about him.

"There now, don't cry! I'm not going to hurt you. Whatever is your name and how do you happen to be here? Where do you live?"

"P-Peter—I'm Peter, an' I d-don't live anywhere—" Sobs made the words sound jerky and run together. "I—I haven't any home!"

"But you must live somewhere," Jim insisted, "Everybody does!"

"But I don't."

"Look now, you'd better tell me why you're here, trying to get into our root cellar." Jim drew his breath in sharply. "So you're the one who broke into the cellar last night—you must have pretty mean parents—to make you steal things."

"I tell you I haven't any folks. I've been living in the woods for a long time. Then I couldn't find any berries or nuts to eat, so I had to do something."

"But that doesn't make sense!" Jim persisted. Where are your folks, Peter? And—how did you get here anyway?"

"Just let me go. I won't bother you any more, honest!"

"Oh, no, you're going to come in the house and talk. Say, how would you like something good to eat for a change?" Jim flashed the light into the boy's face.

Stark hunger took the place of fear. "Swell!" he gasped.

Jim grasped a shockingly light, limp arm of the other boy and helped him to the porch steps, where he seated him. "Be quiet now," he murmured, then ran quickly, but quietly, up the steps, across the porch and into the kitchen. Tiptoeing into the pantry, he picked up the first thing he could find—a big slice of the cake he'd baked yesterday. When he got back to the boy, he found him sobbing again, but softly.

"Here, eat this." Jim put the plate on his lap. "It's the first thing I could find in the dark."

Peter snatched the food offered and wolfed it down in six huge bites.

"You'll have to come inside," Jim said, after the boy had finished. "You can't stay out here in this cold. Come on, but be quiet, we don't want to wake anybody up!"

The stranger seemed grateful as he tottered into the kitchen. Jim moved a chair near the stove. The boy sat down, letting the cozy warmth penetrate his scanty and ragged clothing. The flickering flames lighted up the hollows in his sensitive face and brought out its sharp angles.

Jim disappeared into the pantry again, soon to return with a saucepan filled with homemade soup. He put this on the stove to warm and presently a fragrant smell curled appetizingly into the room.

With a big bowl of soup in one hand and a dish of crackers in the other, Jim motioned to Peter, with a jerk of his head, to follow him.

Once in his bedroom, he knew it would be safe to

whisper. With the door shut, they wouldn't wake his father and brothers.

The fire in the fireplace was low, but a fresh birch chunk soon crackled and sparkled, making a bright light for the pair. They sat on the big bear rug and Jim waited patiently until Peter had finished eating.

The warm soup, the cheerful fire and Jim sitting close by obviously made the younger boy relax. When he had swallowed the last mouthful of food, he breathed a deep sigh of relief. It had been three months since he'd had his last cooked food, he confessed.

Finally, Jim could stand the suspense no longer. "Well, now will you tell me what this is all about? How did you get here? Did you run away from home? Are you trying to play Tarzan?"

The reply was whispered. "I'm nine years old—" His chin quivered a little, but he continued, "Duke brought me here. He'd been taking care of me. We came to the island last summer to fish. One morning when I woke up, he was gone. He took all our food and our boat." Sobs welled up in his throat, but he swallowed and began again. "He always told me not to trust anybody—that they were just a pack of liars and thieves—but I didn't think he'd run away and leave me all alone!"

"Don't you have any mother or father?" Jim asked. "Or sisters or brothers? Or anybody? And who is Duke?"

"No." Peter rubbed his eyes with the back of his hand. "Duke just took care of me."

"Golly, I can't understand why he'd do a thing like that. Weren't you scared, out in the woods all alone?"

"Sure I was scared, but what good did it do me? I went in my tent when it got dark and stayed there. Duke did leave me the tent at least—and the cot. Guess he couldn't take that 'cause I was sleeping on it."

"Where did you come from? You certainly must have some friends some place!"

"No one who'd care where I am. The only family I ever knew were Mr. and Mrs. Carey, in Evansburg, Ohio. They adopted me from the All Saints' Orphanage when I was two years old. They got awful sick last winter and both died of the flu. I loved them both more than anything. They were all alone and I was too, until they adopted me." He paused, then continued, "I was scared when the police couldn't find anyone that I belonged to. They said something about faulty records. I don't know what they meant." Peter struggled with fresh tears, then he went on. "I couldn't stay at the farm alone, so when Duke left, he took me with him." When Jim raised his eyebrows questioningly at the mention of Duke, Peter explained, "He was the hired man."

"That's sure tough, Peter." It wasn't all quite clear yet to Jim but he could see that the exhausted boy was blinking hard to keep awake. "You can curl up here on the rug till tomorrow and we'll see what my dad has to say. He'll know what to do in a case like this."

Jim took the heavy comforter off the bottom of his bed and an extra pillow out of the clothes closet and tucked Peter in for the rest of the night. Before he had finished, the boy was fast asleep.

Jim was just waking up the next morning when Mr. St. Cyr came to the door of his bedroom to call him. He saw his father stare at the small body sprawled out on the bear rug in front of the fireplace.

"Don't wonder you look so surprised, Dad. I'll explain as soon as I get dressed. I'll be right out!" As his father turned and walked toward the kitchen, the bewildered expression still on his face, Jim spoke reassuringly to Peter, who had stirred uneasily under the comforter.

"Don't be scared. Dad's the best person on earth. But you can't blame him for being startled to see you here!" At that moment, Chuck and Jack appeared in the doorway.

"What's this?" Jack demanded curiously. "A hotel?"

"Don't be funny!" Jim told him sternly. He knew how uneasy their strange visitor must be feeling. "This poor boy was half starved, so he was trying to get some food out of the root cellar last night and I heard him." Turning to Peter, he asked, "How do you feel this morning, young fellow?"

"Gee," Peter smiled shyly, "I'd forgotten what a fire felt like. I don't even remember going to sleep. I've been so cold these past nights that I couldn't sleep."

Chuck still stood round-eyed, mouth open, "Where's your house? I don't remember seeing you on the island before. Don't you have any wood to burn?"

"Chuck!" Jim snapped, "Don't be so nosey!"

"Aw heck, I was just askin'." Chuck went back to his room and started to dress.

Jim turned to Jack. "Think you can rustle up some duds for Peter? You two must be about the same size—except for the meat!" He grinned at Peter. "Come on, I'll show you where to wash up. Then we'll talk to Dad."

Before Peter stripped off his tattered clothes, he fumbled in his pocket, brought out a dented little mouth organ and banged some sand from it into the palm of his hand.

While he was taking a shower, Jack, acting on Jim's order, hunted up some clean clothes for the stranger to put on. He came back shortly with a complete outfit.

Peter called from the shower. "Boy, does this hot water feel swell! It's been too cold to take a bath in the Lake lately, anyway. That's what I did in the summertime. Wow! My hair's a mess. It's so snarled I can't even comb it."

But Jim was ready for any emergency. "You leave that to me. I'll fix you up." Taking a pair of scissors from the top drawer of the linen cabinet, he instructed, "Stand still now, and I'll give you the Jim St. Cyr Special!"

He began to cut straight across the back of Peter's hair, from ear to ear. "Now at least you can comb it and it won't look so wild. Dad can finish it. He's quite a barber!"

With the long hair gone and the dirt scrubbed off, Peter made a much better appearance, but the hollows in his cheeks would round out only with plenty of rest and good food. That would take time. Now he stepped hesitantly into the kitchen behind Jim—but he lifted his chin resolutely.

Mr. St. Cyr smiled reassuringly at their young guest. "Well, well, you don't look like the same person. A little soap and water sure makes a big difference." He pointed to a place at the table. "Breakfast's ready—have a chair."

"But I—I" Peter stammered.

"Never mind," the Ranger broke in. "We have plenty of time to talk after we eat. I never could think on an empty stomach."

For a few minutes, only the sound of cutlery and china could be heard. Peter ate as if famished, while Chuck and Jack hardly took their eyes off him.

Jim observed to himself, "The kid has good manners anyway!" But he said nothing.

After breakfast, Mr. St. Cyr told Chuck to help Jack clear off the table, then led Jim and Peter to the living room.

"Now," he began, "let's have it. What happened last night?"

Jim told him the story as Peter had related it to him. The Ranger just sat quietly and listened. Once in a while he glanced at Peter in mingled disbelief and pity. Jim watched the many expressions flit across his father's face as he talked.

"So you see, Dad, he was hungry and cold and tired, or he wouldn't have tried to break in again. Golly, what can we do?"

"You'll have to let me think about this. It's utterly unbelievable that a man in his right mind would do a thing like that to a small boy." He carefully tamped his pipe.

Peter clenched his thin hands. "But I don't think he was in his right mind, Mr. St. Cyr. He never would have left me—I know it—we were pals—" Sobs choked him and he turned away his head. After a while, he continued. "Duke acted kind of funny after he hurt himself. He'd look at me sometimes like he'd never seen me before."

"What do you mean, hurt himself?" the Ranger questioned.

"Oh, he hurt himself one day when we were taking a walk through the woods. He slipped on the edge of a big hole and fell in," Peter explained.

"You mean one of those mine pits?" the Ranger asked.

"Maybe it was a mine pit, I don't know; but anyway, it sure was deep. He cut his head," he pointed his finger at his hairline, "up here."

Mr. St. Cyr frowned. "Could he have lost his memory, do you think?"

Peter seemed to be considering this carefully. "Maybe —he sure acted as if he'd forgotten where we were. The next night he left . . . while I was asleep. I haven't seen him since."

"Until we find out more about this, you can stay here with us. You can go to school with the boys and, in the meantime, I'll see what I can discover." The Ranger blew out a puff of smoke, then seemed lost in thought.

Peter looked at Jim, then back at Mr. St. Cyr. "You mean—You mean—"

"Sure, Peter, think of all the fun you and the boys can have together, while I'm finding out where Duke went. We'll fix up a bunk for you in with Jack and Chuck. Say, I think it would be a good idea if we hiked over to your tent today and looked around."

"I don't want to go back there. I don't ever want to see that place again." Peter's eyes pleaded with the Ranger. "I've looked and looked all around the tent but there's nothing there . . ." The boy's shoulders drooped, obviously at the very thought of the terrible months he'd spent alone.

"It won't hurt to look anyway," Jim offered. "Sometimes you can find things in a spot where you've looked a dozen times before. You're not afraid to go back, are you?"

Peter was, however; he answered, "Not exactly—but can't we wait?"

"Okay," Jim agreed and smiled reassuringly at the boy as they walked back to the kitchen, where Chuck was talking to his pet.

Jim's mind whirled. Was Peter actually afraid to return to the clearing where he'd camped with Duke, or was it only because he was too tired to care what happened? The older boy's thoughts shifted back and forth. He could inquire of his radio friends if they'd seen anyone answering to Duke's description. But now there was no way of leaving the island, unless they sent Peter back with the herders when they took the moose off. But if they did send Peter back to the mainland, where would they send him?

6

wwv • wwv • wwv • wwv • wwv • wwv • wwv

Routine work and chores kept the St. Cyrs busy for the next few days. By the time they had to start school, Jack's leg was well enough to get around on quite nimbly, and the cut in his head had healed. Peter seemed practically one of the family and he and the two younger St. Cyrs had become fast friends. So far, they'd found out nothing whatever about Duke.

Jim had had no opportunity to broach the subject of radio school again to his father. He had hoped that by constant hints he could wear that devoted Ranger down, but he'd been too busy helping get the stores moved to their winter bins and keeping up his daily schedules with his radio friends even to try that tactic. Besides that, his father had been away from the cabin a lot, keeping track of the moose herd so that when the herders came from the mainland, they wouldn't have to hunt up the animals. Jim had no intention of giving up his dream, though.

❂ ❂ ❂

On the appointed Monday morning, Jim was actually anxious to start school and the younger boys were eager to see Miss Gene again.

It wasn't until the following Friday afternoon that Jim had a chance to talk to Miss Gene alone. She had dismissed the children for a short recess and Jim stayed behind to talk to her.

He didn't quite know how to begin, but at last he stammered, "Will—will you give me your opinion on something, Miss Gene?"

She looked at him a bit surprised, then answered, "Well—I will if I can, Jim. What's on your mind?"

"It's like this . . ." Jim's forehead crinkled in perplexity. "I want to go to the mainland next summer—to Michigan Tech, to be exact—but Dad thinks I should stay here and help him. But, golly, I don't want to be a Ranger. I want to be an engineer!"

"And you want me to tell you that you're right and your father is wrong?" Miss Gene asked with a smile as she busied herself with papers on her desk.

Jim shook his head. "No, not exactly. But don't you think that a fellow should be allowed to pick his own future? I do!"

He looked earnestly at his teacher. Obviously, she didn't want to say too much but he wasn't to be put off. "Well—?" the boy insisted.

"I don't quite know what to say, Jim. Does your father know how very much you want to go to radio school?"

"Sure, he knows. But he doesn't understand why I don't want to be a Ranger. He thinks we all should want to do just what he's done all his life." Despair filled Jim's voice.

"But he must have some reason for his stand, Jim. I don't think your father would be unfair."

"I thought maybe—well—oh, heck! I thought you might say something to him, if you get a chance."

"If I ever have an opportunity to talk to him about it, I'll see what I can do," Miss Gene assured him. "But I might do more harm than good."

"It couldn't be any worse than it is now. By the way, Dad said we might ask you to dinner Sunday. Will you come?"

"I'd love to!" Miss Gene's face lighted with eagerness. The late afternoon sun turned her golden hair to a misty halo. "What time do you have dinner, or may I come and help?"

"Come any time you want to after nine o'clock. We don't eat till around three. We might be able to take a hike Sunday morning and show you a bit of our island. Would you like that?" Jim asked.

"Wonderful!" she exclaimed. "I planned to take a walk Sunday, anyway, to see what botany specimens I can collect." She leaned eagerly forward across her desk as she explained, "I specialized in that at college. I studied rock formations, too, and would like to study some of the strata here."

"Golly!" Jim had developed a bad case of teacher worship. "We do lots of collecting, too, only we collect Indian relics. You know, this island has a sort of mysterious background." He edged his chair closer to the desk.

"Mysterious? What's so mysterious about it?" Miss Gene was all attention now and the children outside played on, wondering about the long recess.

"In the first place, the expedition that came here never

could find proof that the Indians were the first people on the island," Jim explained, Miss Gene's interest helping him to forget his shyness. "Some historians say that there are evidences in some of the mines that date from the time of the mound builders or maybe even before."

"Yes, I've read that in books, too, but go on." Miss Gene's voice was warm with enthusiasm.

"There're scientists who think the first inhabitants might have been Norsemen or the Aztecs; but I think that's kind of farfetched, don't you?" Jim asked seriously.

"I don't know enough about it, Jim. Isn't it fascinating, though? Where did you learn all this?"

Jim ran his hand through his crisp red hair as his thoughts went back. "I sort of hung around the fellows in the expedition. You know, some of the pottery they found at a camp site at Chippewa Harbor was like the work of the Iroquois Indians, with some Algonquin and some Sioux." Jim took another deep breath. "They never did decide whether all three races visited the island or if they could have been among the miners at the pits."

Before Miss Gene could answer, Chuck ran into the room. "Is school over for the afternoon, Miss Gene?" he asked. His cheeks were rosy from the crisp, fresh air.

"Oh, goodness! I'm sorry, Charles." Miss Gene jumped up from her chair and hurried outside.

The children had been having too much fun to calm down right away. Making the most of their opportunity to play together, the boys and girls had a variety of games in progress. Due to distance, their chance to congregate only came on school days and on occasional planned celebrations, such as Halloween, Christmas or a school picnic. Miss Gene finally managed by telling them about the

Indian tribes which had lived in the vicinity of Isle Royale.

At the end of school, as Jack, Peter and Chuck were putting on their coats, Jim spoke to them. "You kids run along. I'll catch up with you."

"Don't forget to ask Miss Gene," Jack whispered loudly as he started for the door.

"I did already," Jim answered; then, seeing the question on his brother's face, added, "Yes, she'll come!"

"Oh, boy, swell!" Jack cried and ran to catch up with Peter and Chuck.

Miss Gene turned from waving good-by to the last of her pupils and said to Jim, "I suppose I'd better wear slacks Sunday."

"That'd be best. If we go over to the Monument or to Suzan's Cave, there'll be some climbing to do; that is, if you want to see anything worth while." Jim explained to her in his earnest way. "And the trail is rocky and hard on the feet, so wear boots if you have them!"

"Slacks and boots it will be, then. I certainly don't want to miss anything."

"And don't forget to speak to Dad if you get the chance, please, Miss Gene," Jim reminded her from the doorway.

"I won't forget, Jim. Good-by till Sunday, and thank you all a million for the invitation." There was a smile on her face as she started out for the home of the Reed family, where she was staying.

The next day, Saturday, everything in the St. Cyr home was swept and polished until not a particle of dust was to be seen. By nine o'clock that evening, Roger and the boys were all sitting in front of the fireplace in the younger boys' room, swapping stories and popping corn. A big pan of chocolate was warming on the iron kettle holder. Mr. St. Cyr had made a huge plateful of sandwiches for their supper, and now the five were enjoying the last leisurely hours of their very busy day.

"Where do you think we should go tomorrow?" Jim asked finally. "How about Suzan's Cave or the Monument?"

"How about some of the Indian pits?" Jack asked and wondered why they all laughed.

"I should think you'd have had your fill of pits for a while," kidded Jim.

But their father broke in before the discussion went any further. "I think we'll make the Cave trip. That's not too far and Miss Gregory'll get a kick out of it. She's probably never seen anything like it." He spoke enthusiastically, for he enjoyed a day of collecting as much as his children did. "There are lots of good specimens there, if we can find them!"

"Miss Gene collects, too!" Jim told the others knowingly. "She collects plants. And she's interested in geology. I'll bet she'll like Suzan's Cave. There're plenty of rocks all around."

It was finally decided that they would go to the Cave. They would leave as soon as Miss Gene arrived and get back to the house about three o'clock, for dinner.

Instead of lounging around as usual the next morning, Jim got up early and woke the rest of the St. Cyrs and Peter. By nine o'clock they were all dressed for the trail and ready to leave. A chicken was simmering slowly on the back of the stove. By the time the kitchen fire burned itself out, the chicken would be done. When they reached home, it wouldn't take long to stir up a batch of biscuits. Lettuce, kept crisp and fresh in the still cold of the root cellar, would be fixed in a salad. Carrots, sliced thin, were waiting in water, all set to cook while the biscuits were popped into the oven.

Jim told Chuck to keep watch at the window. At nine forty-five, the small boy yelled, "Here she comes. Gee! Does she look nice?" Hill Billy, frightened by this sudden outburst, ran and sat on top of the door ledge, making funny, squirrel noises.

Everyone went out on the porch to greet the teacher. As soon as the hubbub had subsided, the Ranger suggested that they get started, warning, "It'll take us about an hour to get to the Cave and it's a rocky trail." Then, noticing her stout leather boots, he added, "Good thing you wore heavy boots, Miss Gregory. There's apt to be a bit of rough going."

"Jim warned me Friday that I'd need them," she replied, with a smile at Jim, "and I brought some specimen containers in this!" She held up a small knapsack, filled with little cardboard boxes.

Golly, Jim thought, I sure hope she gets a chance to say something to Dad about radio school!

In a few minutes, they were well along on the rocky path. Steep slopes made the walking even harder and, at some points, the Ranger and Jim went ahead and helped the others up over the boulders.

Wild creatures walked calmly across their path and, at first, Miss Gene seemed timid about them, but as they casually continued on their way, she soon became accustomed to them and, instead of being disturbed, stopped frequently to watch them.

Each new plant the teacher saw was carefully picked and placed in a container. Nearly all the flowers were gone, but in one particular spot, under a low hanging ledge of lava rock, protected from the snow and cold by brush and heavy moss and heated slightly through some strange warmth emanating from small crevices, they found a beautiful devil's club. Jim picked it and handed it to her.

"This plant is familiar in the Pacific Northwest," she cried in amazement, "but that's hundreds of miles from here and far from its natural source!"

"Here's another, Miss Gene. Look! Oh, boy, there's sure a bunch of stuff here!"

"Oh, Jim!" Miss Gene squealed. "Those are Canadian violets—and look—" Her voice broke with excitement. "Here's a ram's head lady's slipper! Rare! Oh—my golly! JIM!"

"This is just like a hot house—a natural one."

"But we shouldn't be finding violets now—" Miss Gene took the plants tenderly from his hands—"These are of the Orchis family and thrive only in the lower swampy lands and bogs!"

"Yes—they do?" Jim's eyebrows lifted in amused denial.

They found innumerable ferns, fungi, mosses and bunchberries. Miss Gene explained the species to them. There were rock brake, bracken, slender cliff brake, fragrant shield fern, fragile fern and others whose names she couldn't remember. There was a deep carpet of trailing juniper in some of the crevices they passed. There was panic grass and mountain rice and bog bilberry peeking out at them from rock ledges and crevices. Each new plant was carefully placed in a container and the name written on a small bit of tape on the top of the box.

By the time they reached Suzan's Cave, Miss Gene's cases were full. Many of the plants were unknown to her and she said she had enough to keep her busy for a week, cataloging them.

Jim explained to her that the cave was located on one of the many sea terraces formed when the island emerged from Lake Superior. "We've explored the Cave lots of times," he said, "and we've found all sorts of relics inside. Someone long ago must have used the place as a sort of shelter. I wonder who it could have been."

Miss Gene scuffed at the deep mat of silt on the floor of the cave.

"I know there's probably nothing much buried underneath the floor of the Cave," Jim suggested, "but let's dig, anyway. There might be some arrowheads or something!"

The Ranger had found a pointed stick and had already started to scratch around with it. Peter, who had become his devoted follower, went to work with a will, too. Miss Gene and Jim followed suit.

Jack and Chuck stood watching. All this extra, uncalled-for exertion didn't appeal to them.

The four dug for a few minutes in silence.

"I guess I was using my imagination too much," Miss Gene remarked, as she sat back for a minute to rest, "but this is a natural preservative and if there's anything under these layers of dirt, it should be in good condition."

Suddenly, there was an exclamation from Jim, who had continued to dig. "I've hit a rock, I think!" He reached down into the hole and lifted out a fairly large piece of stone.

Miss Gene brushed it off. "This seems as if it might be something interesting. Look!"

They all crowded around and examined the rock.

Jim declared, "Looks sort of glassy, doesn't it, Dad?"

The Ranger studied the strange rock. "Yes, I believe we've really found something important. This is a piece of obsidian point. And it *is* glassy! That's the chief characteristic of obsidian." He looked at Miss Gene strangely. "But there's no obsidian on this island!"

"I thought there was supposed to be none closer than Yellowstone Park. How in the world could this have cropped up way over here?" Miss Gene wondered aloud. "This is going to provide an absorbing mystery to try to clear up this winter."

With that, everybody set to, digging with a will but nothing else unusual turned up, so enthusiasm began to lag.

"If anyone is interested, I'm getting hungry," Jim said after a while. "How's about starting for home?" He had begun to realize that Miss Gene could never speak to his father about his future plans with the three younger boys around and decided that, the quicker they headed for the cabin, the more chance she'd have to talk privately.

"I think that's a good idea, Jim. What do you think, Miss Gene? Hungry?" the Ranger asked.

"Now that I stop to think about it, yes," she answered. "Maybe we'd better start before we dig up anything else, then I'd not want to leave at all!"

"I think we'll take the shore trail back," Mr. St. Cyr

said. "It's about the same distance and we can travel a little faster."

Jim took the lead down trail and, once on the shore, he started off briskly, the three boys at his heels, with Miss Gene and his father bringing up the rear.

Looking back over his shoulder several times during the walk toward home, he could see Miss Gene talking earnestly to his father and he could hear the murmur of their voices occasionally, but he couldn't make out what they were saying. He hoped Miss Gene had found a good opening to talk about his going away to radio school next summer. He wondered if she could make his father understand how important it was to him to be able to pick out his own future.

They didn't do any more exploring until they were about a quarter mile from the cabin. Jim halted when Chuck yelled, "Here's where I play sometimes, Miss Gene. Lots of animals come down here to drink. I call it 'My Cove.' See all the pretty rocks I found around here." He pointed to a small pile of stones.

To please him, Miss Gene went over to inspect them.

Suddenly she cried. "Mr. St. Cyr, do come here!" Her voice had an urgent ring to it. "Will you look at this? Do you see what I see, or am I seeing things?"

Jim looked at the stone over his father's shoulder. The latter explained, "It's a green stone gem! Semi-precious. Nothing to get excited about. There are lots of them around on the ground here."

"Aren't they quite valuable?" She took the stone from him and examined it closely.

Jim answered for his father. "Oh, we got all excited

over them once. It's the only semi-precious stone that comes from Michigan, but they're not worth much."

"I'm going to take a couple back with me, anyway. I'd like to have one polished!" She pushed a stray golden lock back off her face. "Well, let's go. Is it very far now? I'm getting weary. I'm not used to so many wonderful discoveries at one time."

Jim mumbled to himself, "The only discovery I want just now is how to make Dad change his mind!"

It was four o'clock by the time they reached the cabin.

The kitchen fire had burned long enough to cook the chicken to a delicious tenderness and Jim started a fresh fire. "I'll make the biscuits," he offered, "and you kids set the table!"

"Let me help." Miss Gene followed Jack to the cupboards and began to set the table. "I believe I've walked up an appetite!" Everyone laughed.

"Me, too!" Chuck hung back, as the teacher took over his usual job.

By the time that Jim's biscuits were a golden brown, everything else was ready and waiting.

"Here we are," He opened the oven door, and pulled out a large pan of hot biscuits. "Sit down, everyone."

Two hours passed before the meal was over and the dishes were again in the cupboard, washed and dried by the boys.

"I'll have to get back," Miss Gene spoke reluctantly from her chair beside the fireplace. "It's wonderful to sit back and see boys doing dishes!" She grinned at the Ranger, who sat across from her, on the other side of the fireplace.

"Dishes!" Chuck snorted.

Jack laughed at the face he made. "Well, I guess there're lot's of things worse than dishes—though right now I can't think what."

"Never mind," Jim spoke from his sprawled-out position on the bear rug. "We're lucky we have dishes and something to dirty them with."

"*Hmmm*, a philosopher!" His father chuckled.

Miss Gene rose from her chair, slowly, like a lazy kitten rises after a bowl of milk and a nap. "I've had a perfectly wonderful day. But all good things do end—you know."

The sun was painting the western sky a riot of flame and orange as they left the cabin.

"Shall we take the beach trail, it's much shorter?" Jim asked as they started out.

"Good idea," his father answered and they all turned toward the beach. It took a half hour of steady walking to reach the Reed home.

"Good night, and thanks for a perfect day." Miss Gene grasped the Ranger's hand for a brief moment.

"It sure was fun," Jack told her.

"Sure was—" Jim spoke softly, a tinge of disappointment in his voice.

"Bye." Chuck's pleased grin was more expressive than his conversation.

As the St. Cyrs and Peter retraced their steps homeward in the increasing darkness, Jim made up his mind to ask his father about radio school again, himself.

"I've been thinking about next summer, Dad." He spoke after they'd gone some distance in silence. "I talked to the operator over at Houghton, and he said the College of Mines is offering a scholarship in radio. Golly! Would

I ever like to win that!" Jim's eyes sparkled at the very thought of what this would mean.

Mr. St. Cyr glanced sharply at the tall boy who strode beside him. "I thought we'd settled that argument once and for all!" He sounded annoyed. "I said you couldn't go over to the radio college next summer and that's final. What would I do here without you to help me?"

"But, Dad—" Jim hesitated, then plunged ahead. "Jack's old enough now to look after things at the cabin, and, anyway, he likes it better than I do!" The boy's heels struck angrily on the stony beach and the stench of rotting fish and seaweed rose sharply into his nostrils.

"Jack is only nine!" his father retorted.

"But I was only twelve when Mother died and I've been taking charge at the cabin ever since! Jack knows far more now at nine than I did then, and I got along all right," Jim argued bitterly. Probably Miss Gene hadn't had a chance to put in a good word for him. It certainly didn't look it.

"That's neither here nor there! You're needed at home. I couldn't leave the cabin for long if the boys were alone, so how would I get my work done?" his father doggedly tried to explain, but Jim was too angry to reply.

The rest of the walk was made in silence, Jim with a frown on his forehead and his father with a stern, tight look around his lips. Jack, Peter and Chuck had been too busy playing along the trail to pay any attention to the argument.

7

vvvv • vvvv • vvvv • vvvv • vvvv • vvvv • vvvv

Jim trudged dejectedly out to his radio shack. He could figure no possible solution to his all important problem. He pushed open the door, threw his cap on the daybed in the corner of the room and looked around at his radio cards and radio gear. There was deep pride etched strongly in the set of his chin and on his high forehead at what he saw.

He flipped the filament switch on the transmitter and eased into the comfortable chair before his desk.

The transmitter tubes began to glow as he tuned the receiver to 3900 and heard "Calling CQ, calling CQ, calling CQ, W9XXM, Houghton, Michigan, calling CQ and standing by. Come in some one, please."

"*Hum*—just in time," Jim murmured as he turned on the plate switch and started his answer.

"Calling W9XXM, calling W9XXM, W9XXM. How about it, Tom? This is W9ZZO, Isle Royale, calling you and standing by. Come in please."

"9XXM back to 9ZZO. Hi! How's the boy tonight? Was hoping you'd be on the air. I've got news for you. One of the teacher's pets is slated for that scholarship, I guess. Heard one of the fellows telling about it just a little while ago. Tough luck, kid! But I'll keep you posted on any new developments. What's new over on the island? W9XXM, over."

"W9XXM, this is W9ZZO. Okay, Tom. Guess that about washes me up. Dad doesn't approve, anyway. Suppose I'll have to forget about it. Kind of figured that I'd stand some chance if I could have taken the tests. I've been studying pretty hard the last few months. Say— what's that fellow's name? I mean the one who's getting the scholarship? Over."

"I don't know his name, Jim. I'll let you know more about it later. They're having some kind of board meeting tomorrow and I think the newspapers will have it then. They've hired a couple new 'Profs,' too. Say, how about a game of checkers tonight? We never did finish that last game we were playing. Did you make that new board? W9XXM over."

"I'll be anxious to hear more about it," Jim returned. "At that board meeting, well, they might change their minds about giving the scholarship to that guy! Yup, I made the new board but I don't feel like a game of checkers tonight. Sorry, pal. Maybe tomorrow night. See you then, ol' man. S'long. W9ZZO signing off and clear with W9XXM."

Next morning, as Jim walked to school with the three younger boys, he decided that he'd talk with Miss Gene and find out if she really hadn't said anything to his father yet. By the way his father had answered him last night, he felt pretty sure that the teacher couldn't have had a chance to try to put in a word for him.

After the rest of the children had filed out for morning recess, Jim slowly approached Miss Gene's desk. His face reddened a bit and he dug his hands deep into his pockets as he stood, first on one foot then the other.

"Did you say anything to Dad, Miss Gene?" he finally blurted out.

The teacher sat gazing out of the window. "Not exactly —that is, I decided to think it over before saying anything to him." She leaned forward on her elbows. "I don't quite know how to say this; but don't you think you should wait a year, Jim?"

The boy gave her one long look of bitter disappointment and stalked out of the schoolroom. He'd been so sure that she would see his point of view, but she, too, sided against him. It wasn't fair! Did they all expect him to stay home for years and take care of his brothers?

He walked to the ridge and sat down on a log to think. One of the boys called to him to come and play hand-ball but he paid no attention to him.

The bell rang to call the children in and he walked slowly back to the schoolroom. For the rest of the day he recited automatically and brushed aside every overture Miss Gene made to break his frozen attitude.

While the children were getting on their coats to go home, Miss Gene called to him. "Jim, may I see you for a moment before you leave?"

He stood in the doorway of the cloakroom and answered stiffly, "Yes."

Miss Gene began, "I hope I didn't hurt your feelings, Jim. I only meant to be helpful."

"I thought maybe you'd try to make Dad see things my way," he answered bitterly. "I'm not kicking about my life so far. It's been wonderful. But I don't want to be a Forest Ranger and I don't want to stay on this island for-ever, either." He put up his hand as she tried to interrupt him. "Living on the island has been swell, but I wish Dad could see that I'm not cut out to be a Ranger. Well—good-by—and thanks, anyway." Turning, he almost ran out of the room, the stubborn, strong swing of his shoul-ders a perfect, unconscious imitation of his father.

He caught up with Jack, Peter and Chuck when they were climbing to the top of the ridge and stalked along beside them, only half listening to their chatter. . . .

Mr. St. Cyr's greeting was jovial as Jim threw open the kitchen door.

"Hello, boys! Come in! Come in! Don't stand there with the door open. I want you to meet the round-up crew."

Motioning to the two young men seated at the table, the Ranger introduced them. "Meet Red Cory and Tim Sullivan. They came over on the Coast Guard cutter this afternoon."

Jim, Jack and Peter, all said at the same time, "Hello," while Chuck eyed the strangers carefully, then said, "Hi!" Hill Billy made a mad dash for the top of the door-sill.

From the living room, Jim listened to the murmur of voices as the two men discussed the different ways of trapping moose with his father. Jack nudged him and whispered, "I wonder how they'll ever catch the moose? Gee! I hope we can watch them some day."

Jim grinned and Chuck piped up excitedly, "Me, too! Looks like they're going to stay here with us."

Before Jim could answer, his father called from the kitchen. "The cutter dropped a mail sack for us, too, and there seems to be a lot of mail—including a few packages. I've got it here on the table. Come and get it!"

Jim's stack of mail proved to be enormous—a huge pile of radio QSL cards from stations he'd worked over the air and two packages. He opened the largest box first. It was a Hallicrafter Sky Chief radio receiver. All he could do was swallow hard several times. "Gosh," he thought to himself, "maybe I'm wrong at that. Dad sure does the darndest things for me, right when I think he's against me." To his father he said aloud, "It's just super, Dad!"

By this time, the other boys had stopped exclaiming over their share of mail, and Jim watched the expressions on their faces as they opened their packages.

Jack's pile consisted of some catalogs and mail from advertisements he'd answered, and a box about fifteen inches square.

Chuck had two boxes, one like Jack's and another smaller one.

Jack pulled and tugged at the tape that sealed the square box and at last got it open. It was a compact, six-tube radio. His surprise and enthusiasm seemed enough thanks for his father. But his breathless, "Gee, Pop, this is swell—" brought a quiet smile to Mr. St. Cyr's face.

Peter's box contained a complete outfit, from underclothing to a bright new cap and a sturdy pair of boots. The tears in his eyes made the Ranger look away as he mumbled, "Thanks," around the lump in his throat.

Chuck opened his larger box and lifted out an exact duplicate of Jack's radio. He threw himself into his fa-

ther's arms. "Honest, Dad, is it really for my very own?"
he asked over and over.

Roger St. Cyr laughed. "Yes, of course. These radios
will be a lot of fun for you during the winter. They're for
your desks. And for the love of Mike, keep your hands off
my set now!" He explained to Red and Tim, "There're
so many stories they like to hear that it's usually a tossup—
Ranger frequency or thriller! In the middle of an interesting chapter of some serial, I generally have a schedule call
to make or headquarters calls me and that leaves the story
hanging in mid-air!"

Red and Tim laughed at the Ranger's explanation for
his generous gifts, and the youngsters made a hasty exit,
to put their prizes in their bedroom.

Jim had still another package to open. He didn't know
that his father was watching him tensely as he cut the
string on the box.

He fumbled eagerly with the layers of tissue that concealed the object in the box. When the last layer was removed, the smile on his face turned to a momentary
flicker of dismay. His heart dropped sickeningly within
him. He looked up into his father's eyes. "They're nice,
Dad," he said slowly, as he lifted a beautiful pair of ten-
power Ranger field glasses from the box, "but you
shouldn't have spent so much money on them."

His father smiled, the tenseness around his lips soften-
ing for a moment. "I had a chance to get them at a real
bargain and knew you'd be needing them. I've had mine
for a long time, and in our job you can't get along without
them."

Tim and Red fidgeted uncomfortably during the long

pause that followed, as they watched first the Ranger, then Jim.

"They're too expensive for me though, Dad," Jim said finally and, turning slowly, he went on dragging feet out to the radio shack, his new receiver tucked safely under his arm. His father evidently thought that he'd persuaded him to give up the idea of radio school!

When Jim stepped into the cabin a half hour later, supper was ready and on the table. He tousled Jack's hair before they sat down and whispered, "Thanks, kid, for fixing supper, I'll do something for you!"

Jack winked back and answered softly, "Forget it. I guess you must be feeling pretty low, even with the swell presents. Don't worry, maybe we can make Dad change his mind before next spring!"

"Not much chance, I guess," Jim whispered back, his shoulders drooping.

"What're you two cronies whispering about?" Their father called from the pantry. "We're ready to eat."

8

vvvv • vvvv • vvvv • vvvv • vvvv • vvvv • vvvv

It was a few minutes after six before Jim finally got out to the radio shack again. As he warmed up the transmitter, he heard Tom calling from Houghton. At last the transmitter was ready to operate, and Jim flipped the controls and spoke into the microphone.

"W9ZZO calling W9XXM. W9ZZO calling W9XXM—over."

"W9XXM back to W9ZZO. Hi, kid, wondered what had happened. What's cookin'? W9XXM over."

"W9ZZO back to W9XXM. Gee, I'm sorry I couldn't get out here on time—just got through with the dishes. Had the roundup crew for supper, and it took a little longer than I expected. Got your checkerboard ready?"

"W9XXM to W9ZZO. So they really are going to round up some of the moose! I thought you were kidding me. Bet they'll have some fun. Those babies are nothing to monkey with. How're they going to catch 'em? Yup—board's ready. I'll start it out by moving red number one to black number two. Come in, Jim!"

The boys played fast tonight and Tom won the game after a lively bout. "This must be my unlucky day," Jim thought as he signed off.

Two emergency cots had been put up in the kitchen for Red and Tim and they were making them up when Jim entered the cabin. With a cordial but brief "Good night," he crossed to his bedroom and closed the door behind him.

Next morning as they sat at the breakfast table, Jim asked, "How do you plan to catch the moose?"

Red explained, "I guess we'll have to use box traps. We've been trying to figure the best way to do it, and I think that's about the safest. The boat will be over today with our horses—" He grinned at Roger. "And I think the Rangers are sending one for you at the same time." This was a long speech for Red and he promptly turned back to his plate of ham and eggs.

"Oh, goody!" Chuck shouted. "Can we ride him, too?"

His father sounded a bit dubious as he answered, "Well, Son, we'll see what kind of a horse they're sending me. If it's safe, I might let you try it. It's been over six years since I've been on a horse myself, so I won't promise!"

Jim looked inquiringly at Red. "Will we be able to go along some day while you're at work here? I'd like to see how you catch those big fellows."

"It's dangerous business, but maybe you can string along one day. It depends! We might need an extra hand and you seem to be a pretty husky specimen."

Jim had stepped over to refill his coffee cup from the big pot on the range and he did look handsome and fit as he stood there, his six-foot frame, straight and strong, topped with a thick thatch of curly, red hair.

"Any time you say," he answered with a grin. "We redheads must stick together!" He glanced at his watch. "We'd better scram for school, kids! It's ten minutes after eight now." He drank his second cup of coffee standing up and grabbed his heavy mackinaw from its hanger. "So long, Dad. Good-by, fellows. See you later!"

Although Miss Gene tried to talk to Jim during the morning, he sat quietly preoccupied, answering only when called upon to recite and making no effort to enter any other discussions. During the walk home for their noontime meal, he stalked along silently beside the younger boys and paid little attention to what they were saying.

As they came in sight of the cabin they saw several huge boxes out in the clearing. A large ferryboat was tied up at the wharf, where it rocked gently, like a leaf on a millpond. Sounds of confusion reached the boys' ears as they raced down the slope and around to the back of the cabin.

There, tethered to one of the clothesline braces, stood three beautiful horses. One was white, with black feet and a star on his long forehead; one was a pinto; and the third, jet black.

As the boys halted, speechless with delight, the animals turned their heads and looked at them. The white horse curled his nose gently and whinnied softly.

Jim gasped, "Golly, aren't they simply something?"

"Wonder which one's Dad's?" Jack's eyes were snapping with suppressed excitement. Chuck was already scampering up to them, to rub their noses. Peter stood back and watched, his hands gripped tightly together.

"Be careful, Chuck! You don't know whether they'll

like you or not." Jim's advice came much too late. Chuck was already talking softly to the three animals and rubbing their noses. The white horse nibbled lightly at his fingers, as if to say thank you.

Hill Billy gave one shriek and vanished into the treetops. Obviously, the sight of his young master standing beside these monsters frightened him beyond all reason.

The smell of cooking food floated out of the open kitchen window and the boys moved toward the cabin. "Dad must be getting dinner again. Those men must be here yet." Jim sounded glad to relinquish his job as cook for a change.

Mr. St. Cyr, Red and Tim were already seated at the table, eating, when the boys stamped in. The Ranger explained: "We had to get an early start, so I hurried up with the dinner. Jim, will you take the rest of the food off the stove?"

"Sure," Jim answered, "Beautiful horses out there. Which one is yours, Dad?" He voiced Jack's question.

"I hope it's the white one!" Chuck declared, bouncing up and down in his eagerness.

"Why do you say that?" His father stopped eating for a moment, his fork halfway to his mouth. "I suppose you've made friends with them already."

Chuck answered seriously, "The white one sure is wonnerful! She liked to have her nose rubbed!"

"You guessed right, Son; the white one is ours."

"For keeps?"

"*Um-hum,* I think so," the Ranger smiled warmly, "at least for as long as we need her." The white mare would not lack loving care if Chuck had his way.

"What's her name?"

"They didn't tell me in the report and there were no names on the bridles. What would you like to call her?"

"I called her 'Star.' Isn't that a super name?"

The men laughed. "He's one step ahead of you, Roger," Tim said as he pushed his chair away from the table. "I'll go out and get the packs ready. We'd better get going."

Mr. St. Cyr grinned back at Tim over Chuck's head. "The herd is over on Siskowit Lake. I took a run up there this morning, to make sure. It's about two miles on the Siskowit Trail. It won't take long with the horses."

"It's going to be a job, carting those heavy crates up the trail." Tim spoke ruefully. "Back in Montana, when we needed to round up a cow and bring her in, all we had to do was head her for home and ride behind to see that she didn't wander."

"We'll be lucky if we corral one of those monsters, let alone get her down that rocky trail to the boat." Red grimaced.

"Between the three of us, we should be able to get one down every three or four hours. Thank heavens, they don't want the whole herd!" Red snorted. "I never knew I'd end up punching bull moose! Would the boys ever get a kick out of that back home?" Both he and Tim had been raised on a cattle ranch in the West and had volunteered to the Conservation Department, when they'd sent out a call to cattlemen for help.

"Can we stay home this afternoon and watch?" Chuck asked, and a puckish, wistful smile curled the corners of his lips.

"No," his father answered firmly. "Saturday will be time enough for you to watch us. By then, we should know just what we have to do."

Jim had been listening to the conversation without taking part and after his father left, he urged the boys to hurry. "Maybe we'll be able to get home in time to meet them up the trail," he suggested.

School held no interest for the boys that afternoon. The trail home seemed twice as long to their scurrying feet and even Jim felt a bit elated at having something to look forward to besides helping his father with the Ranger duties, but they finally reached the cabin.

The boat at the wharf still rode the long swells. A deep silence hung thickly over the clearing.

"Let's go up the trail to meet them," Jim suggested.

"Let's!" Quickly Jack and Chuck and Peter agreed.

The rocky, slippery trail led past Lake Whittlesey and sometimes reached almost to the shore line itself. The boys walked quickly along the path. At one point, where they could see the Lake, a large flock of Canadian geese rose, honking, into the clear, crisp air, to disappear into the north.

Spruce trees, some of the largest ones twenty inches in diameter, grew up from a green bed of rattlesnake fern and bristly gooseberry. Yellow birch, fat and squatty from the short summer seasons, curled their long roots into the hard soil, digging deep to find food.

Suddenly Jim, who was in the lead, held up his hand.

"Listen, I hear something coming down the trail!" They all heard the pounding noise.

All at once he yelled, "Duck!" Leaping at the three smaller boys, he gave them a push that landed them plump into a bed of skunk cabbage, and threw Hill Billy, who was perched on Chuck's shoulder as usual, off balance into a pile of underbrush.

Just as Jim dived after them, a big black shape galloped along the path where they'd been walking. Directly behind the black streak, lasso whirling, rode Red—his hat dangling by the chin strap and flopping madly against his back.

Close on Red's heels sped Tim and Ranger St. Cyr, their mounts following the flying heels of Red's pinto.

Jim drew a deep breath.

"Wow! Was that a narrow squeak?" He slapped his forehead with the palm of his hand. "Red sure didn't waste any time getting into western roundup action. Guess he must have decided that a cow is still a cow, even if it is a moose!"

Jack and Chuck laughed hysterically, "Nuts to moose!" Chuck gasped, and Jack added, "Let's get out of here before another monster comes along!"

Peter picked himself up out of the middle of the skunk cabbage, wrinkling his nose. "Once is enough for me. I'm not curious any more, thanks."

Jim hooted at the youngsters. "Fine bunch of cowhands you'd make!" But inside he was still shaking at the narrow escape they'd had from serious injury.

He led the way back to the cabin in silence. Hill Billy followed overhead, leaping from branch to branch, still afraid to take another chance of being helped to a flying ride into space.

Alongside the cabin, the three horses were standing quietly munching on some hay, and the moose that had almost run the boys down was on the ground nearby, trussed up. Red and Tim were struggling to tie a sack over its head. They finally managed to get it far enough on to cover the animal's eyes.

The pinto and black horse were led over and placed, one on each side of the winded moose. Then the ropes were slowly loosened on its front legs, from a tight, binding noose to a hobble. As the ungainly animal struggled to its feet, the horses, trained in the art of gentling even a vicious, man-killing stallion,, moved in close to its heaving sides, and the ropes around its neck tightened. There wasn't much the moose could do after that except go where it was led. The strange procession moved slowly along the wharf and the moose was guided into a large crate which stood in the yawning mouth of the hold of the ferry. The blindfold would not be removed until the animal had quieted down. Two other crates with similar occupants told the boys that much had happened while they had been in school.

When the third crate had been secured to Red's satisfaction, he yelled from the boat. "That's all for today, men. I'll be with you in a few minutes."

Mr. St. Cyr and Tim wiped their damp faces and breathed a sigh of relief. "It's worse than I thought it would be," the Ranger declared. "I'll be glad when this is over!"

"Too bad you missed the show, boys. It was exciting, to say the least!"

"I'll just bet it was." Jim looked at the younger boys and winked. It might be just as well not to mention that they'd had ringside seats along the trail, that afternoon.

9

www • www • www • www • www • www • www

Early the next morning Jim heard his father stirring the fire in the range and he wiggled comfortably in his bed. It's Saturday, he thought lazily—then remembered Red and Tim. He could hear them dressing in the kitchen and talking to his father at the same time.

"I certainly enjoyed that sleep last night. How'd you feel this morning after your horseback riding, ol' timer?" Red asked the Ranger.

"Don't even talk about it! I'm so stiff and sore I could hardly crawl out of bed. A guy sure takes a lot of punishment, trying to be more comfortable. I feel like somebody took a half hitch in my spine!" Mr. St. Cyr groaned.

Red and Tim guffawed.

The Ranger looked with envy at the cowpuncher curve that Red and Tim had in their legs. "You sure do fit a saddle nice," he said with a rueful grin. Then he added, "Oatmeal's ready. Guess I can call the boys. It's Saturday morning but I think they'd rather get up than miss anything!"

The three younger boys were already dressed, however. They raced out of their room as Mr. St. Cyr was about to call them. Jim grinned, threw back the bedclothes and stretched. "Might as well get up, too," he murmured as one foot reached over the side and explored for his bedroom slippers.

Right after breakfast, Red and Tim left with their horses. Mr. St. Cyr stayed at home to catch up on his radio reports.

Jim went to the radio shack directly after he finished his morning work, to keep schedules with some of the fellows. He cut these short because he had persuaded Peter to lead the way to where he'd camped with Duke, so they could look around. Within a half hour he was hurrying up the path to the cabin. Jack and Peter came out on the porch to meet him.

"Be ready in a jiff, kids," he said as he took the steps three at a time and disappeared into the kitchen.

Just as the four boys were ready to leave the cabin, they heard the roar of an airplane motor far out over the water.

"Sounds like it's headed this way," declared Jim, shading his eyes to look out over the glistening bay.

"Wonder who it is," responded Jack as he, too, tried to locate the plane.

"I know Dad didn't expect a plane today—he'd have mentioned it. It might be the mail, but if it is, he's early. He's not due here till next Tuesday."

"Well, we'll soon find out! There she comes!" Jack exclaimed.

The aircraft was painted a bright red, with a large American flag decorating the side and its license numbers shimmering on the under-wing, which meant that it was the seaplane sometimes used by the Postal Department to deliver mail to the island.

Coming in at an altitude of about one hundred feet, the pilot leveled out and flew across the clearing once, then did a sharp left bank and came back again.

As he neared the center of the clearing, he opened the door of the trim Taylorcraft and pushed the mail sack out. The attached parachute opened as the wind from the slip stream hit it and the sack floated earthward.

Jim was waiting for it to hit and as he picked it up he said, gently shaking the bag, "Good thing there's no glass in here."

He carried the sack to the kitchen. Emptying the mail on the table he sorted it into neat stacks.

Chuck dashed in with Hill Billy clinging to his shoulder. "Any mail for me?" he asked breathlessly.

"A couple of catalogs . . . oh yes, and a letter, too. Here —catch!" Jim tossed it to him.

Chuck caught the envelope and picked up the catalogs, then turned and skipped into his bedroom, where he curled up on his bunk. Hill Billy leaped to the middle of the big, fat pillow at the head of the bed and crawled inside the open end of the case. Before Chuck could open the letter, which obviously was an advertisement of some sort of animal food, he heard Jim calling, "Come on, kids! I think we'd better leave the mail to read when I get back. If we don't get started now, we won't have time to go at all before lunch."

Handing his father a stack of mail as he sat at the Ranger transmitter, Jim asked if there was anything more for him to do before he left. "We'll be back in a little while. We're going over to Peter's tent and see what we can find!" he explained. "I've finally persuaded him to go back and look around, but it took some doing!"

"Okay, but be back before lunch. If you happen to see a groundnut, bring it home, will you? We haven't had any for a long time."

"Good idea," Jim answered.

Jack and Peter were ready and waiting for him on the porch. Chuck had become absorbed in his precious squirrel colony and could not be lured away. As the three boys started out, Peter murmured, "I hate to go back to that place. Do we have to go?"

When Jim nodded, he asked anxiously, "What did your father say to bring home?"

"A groundnut, didn't you ever eat them?"

"No. Do you mean they grow out in the woods?" Peter's dark eyebrows lifted in surprise.

"Of course! They're lickin' good, too. I like them better than potatoes. You know, if I ever got lost in the woods, I could live on just what I could find to eat."

"I wish I could have. But Jim, do we have to go to the tent?"

"Golly, don't you want to try to find out where Duke went?" Jim couldn't understand the boy's reluctance to return to the tent.

Peter broke in half-fearfully, "You won't find anything around there that'll tell you that! I looked and looked, but couldn't find a single thing."

"Oh, well, you might see something now that you didn't see before, because, when you're used to seeing a thing all the time, it doesn't seem important to you. Remember, too, you were pretty weak and hungry when we found you."

"Gosh," Peter cried, "don't remind me of it!"

It took them a half hour to locate the pitched tent. Peter had forgotten the exact trail he'd taken to reach the cabin.

When they finally found the spot where Duke had encamped with Peter, Jim exclaimed, "This isn't more than a fifteen-minute walk from our place. There's a mine pit near here some place and a sugar grove by the mine where we tapped the trees and caught sap for our last sugar party."

"What's a sugar party?" Peter's eyes were round with curiosity.

"If you stay with us long enough, you'll see what it is," Jack answered.

"We'd better get to work and cover every inch of this clearing," Jim said briskly. "Pick up anything you see that might have some connection with Duke or Peter."

Their search uncovered only a few rusty cans and one battered cooking pan that had been discarded. Finally, they sat down to rest on a fallen log, tired and discouraged.

"Nothing much here, let's go back!" Jack finally suggested. "I'd like to watch Red and Tim catch moose."

"I mustn't forget to look for groundnut," Jim answered, "I'll hunt over by the stream, there might be some nice ones over there."

The two youngsters ran ahead of him to the small stream. "There should be some fish here, too. Did Duke do any fishing while you were here?" Jack asked Peter.

Peter nodded vigorously. "The reason we picked this

place to camp in the first place was because of the stream. We both caught some big rainbow trout. I can still taste them. *Mmmm*—were they good!"

Jim grinned understandingly but said nothing.

"If we had some string, we could maybe catch some fish for dinner. Look inside your pockets," Jack urged Peter. "I think there was some string in that inside pocket of the jacket. I wore that coat to school yesterday and I remember picking some up and sticking it in my pocket."

Peter explored and found a tiny ball of white string. Jack took a pin from his lapel and bent it. With his knife, he dug in the damp, black earth near the base of a maple tree until he found a fat angleworm. He threaded this on the pin and dropped it carefully over the edge of a projecting rock that cast a heavy shadow on the swift, cold stream. It bobbed gaily on the top of the bubbling water.

Jim sat on a log near the river's edge and tossed bits of stick into the rushing water. His thoughts were not on the antics of the two boys as they lay flat on the thick pad of pine needles that covered the cold ground, waiting tensely for a strike.

Suddenly the string jerked tight!

Jack squealed and let out a little more string. The fish struggled at the end of the pin, splashing and leaping, trying to spit it out. At the top of a three-foot leap, the big trout gave an extra flip with his tail and nosed straight down again.

Then the string hung limp.

"Doggone it—look!" Jack held up the string and there dangled the straightened pin.

Peter giggled. "It must have been at least a five-

pounder, by the looks of that pin! I've read about fishing
with a pin—and now I've seen it. I'll take a fishhook for
mine, if I'm hungry!"

"But it works most of the time," Jack objected. "I've
caught lots of fish with a pin! Golly!" His eyes sparkled
and Jim had to grin at the true fisherman's expression on
his brother's face, "It sure was a whopper, wasn't it?"

Peter nodded. "Swell fish story it'll make, too! We can
come back another day and bring some real fishhooks.
That's more fun anyway!"

"Incidentally," Jim broke in on their plans, "it doesn't
happen to be open season on trout. You'd have had to
throw it back anyway!" His laughter filled the little glen
as he saw the looks of consternation on the faces of Jack
and Peter. "But this isn't finding groundnut," he reminded them, uncurling himself from his comfortable
position on the log. "We'd better get going. We'll only
just make it by dinner time now!"

He walked along the river's edge until he came to a
clump of low bushes that hugged the ground. Suddenly
he exclaimed, "Hey, kids! Come here. I've found one.
You can help me dig it out."

"I don't see anything but a bunch of scrub—" Peter declared as he ran to where Jim stood. "Don't tell me you
eat that stuff!"

"No, not the scrub, silly! See that small vine climbing
around back and forth over the brush? Well, that's
groundnut! In the summertime it has a blossom on it.
Looks like a bean blossom!" Jim explained.

"I don't see anything to eat on that thing!" Peter insisted and Jack snorted as Jim continued.

"Of course, you don't see anything. It's all under the ground. Help me dig up the roots."

The two younger boys helped Jim dig and soon they uncovered the root system of the wild bean vine. It had eight fat tubers on it, most of them about three inches in diameter. They were connected to each other by narrow, fibrous strands.

Jack licked his lips. "Yummy! These are much better than potatoes. The Indians used to eat these and Dad said that the Pilgrim Fathers ate them like we eat potatoes, too."

Peter's eyes widened in surprise. "Golly, this is really fun! I didn't know you could find things like this out in the woods."

"Humph," snorted Jim, "you could live all the time on what you could find, if you had to. Great botanists, like —like Asa Gray, said that if the first civilization had started in America, this root would've been cultivated and would have been our potato. They're sweet and you can eat them raw, if you have to. But we all like them cooked or baked best!"

"I wish I'd have known about these when I was so darn hungry. Food like this in my front yard and I didn't even know it." Peter surveyed the clearing with a new interest.

"This is only one of the things you could have found," Jack told him. "If we had more time, I'll bet I could find a dozen things right here that you could live on if you had to." His face lighted with the enthusiasm of a born naturalist as he rattled on. "There are Indian breadroot, Indian cucumber root, hog peanut, mech-mech—another kind of potato root, earth apple—something like an artichoke, wild onion—we call them leeks, and, oh, lots more.

There's a root called calamus that the Indians used to eat to cure stomach-ache and it's used out East as a candy." As he paused for breath, Peter made a face at him.

"You're just kidding me now," he said.

"Nope!" Jack insisted. "You cook the root for a while, then slice it thin and boil it in a thick syrup. It tastes something like candied ginger. We make it sometimes. It's really good." He drew a long breath. When he got wound up on botany, it seemed he just couldn't stop.

"Do you suppose I can learn how to find all those things?" Peter asked.

"If you stay with us, you'll learn lots more than that. We have picnics in the summertime and, once in a while, we don't take anything to eat except our meat. We see what we can collect for dinner, and then cook it over our campfire. It's loads of fun! Dad teaches us woodlore every time we go out. Why, even Chuck could live in the woods if he got lost."

"I often wondered how an Indian could live out in the woods and not have a garden or buy things from a store. Now I see how they could," Peter declared eagerly. "All they needed was a bow and arrow—for meat. The rest just grew!"

Jim couldn't get all steamed up about woodlore, even though he knew as much—perhaps more—than Jack did about it, so he let his brother spout on.

"Gosh, Indians are smart. They can get everything they need right out in the woods. . . . Sometimes I pretend I'm an Indian—"

"We'd better pretend Indians are chasing us and scram out of here as fast as we can. Dad'll wonder where we are." Jim glanced at his watch as he spoke. "Golly, it's dinner time right now!"

The boys scrambled around, stuffing the tubers in their pockets, and then, with Jim in the lead, they trudged single-file down the trail.

As they walked, the sound of an airplane reached them once more. Jim looked overhead, but the trees were so dense, he couldn't see it. "Mail plane again—" was his surprised comment to the younger boys scampering along behind him. "He must have had the long flight today and is on his return trip."

10

vvvvv • vvvvv • vvvvv • vvvvv • vvvvv • vvvvv • vvvvv

Nearing the cabin, Jim and the boys could see that the mail plane was moored to the float. The pilot evidently was still with Mr. St. Cyr. Only one horse, Star, was tethered at the usual place. Red and Tim could not have come back.

Mr. St. Cyr, the pilot and Chuck were finishing their dinner in the kitchen as Jim opened the door. He sniffed and exclaimed, "Does it smell good? Ask me—does it?"

Chuck asked seriously, "Well, does it?" and wondered why they all laughed!

"Found you some groundnut, Dad, and we almost had fish for supper, too. Jack had a great big trout on the hook and the doggoned pin straightened!"

"It's a good thing for him that it did straighten. I'd have had to arrest him for fishing out of season. The fish must have known it." Everyone laughed at Jack's pink face this time. "Put the groundnut over on the table. I'll take care

125

of them later," the Ranger said, then turned to Peter to ask, "Did you find anything at the camp?"

The sad smile on the thin young face was answer enough.

"I'm sorry, lad, but we want you to stay with us as long as you wish."

The pilot rose from the table, saying, "I've got to push on, Roger. Thanks for chow! Now I won't have to eat cold sandwiches out of a lunch box."

"Glad you stayed," the Ranger responded heartily. "Anything we can do—and any time you come, you're more than welcome."

Jack nudged Jim and spoke in an undertone. "Let's go to the float with them before we eat."

Jim nodded agreement. They followed their father and the pilot to the dock and watched the latter untie the pontoons from the float and jump into the cabin of the seaplane.

Suddenly the engines blasted forth in a full-throated roar. At the first burst of sound, Hill Billy made a flying leap from Chuck's shoulder, miscalculated the distance to the timber piling of the pier and landed with a plop in the water.

Chuck screamed, "Help me get Hill Billy—he's in the water!"

Jim ran to the edge of the float, threw himself on his stomach and stretched out his hand to the half-drowned squirrel, while Jack and Peter sat on his legs to hold him down. Hill Billy struggled to reach Jim's hand but couldn't quite make it. Peter yelled, "Take off your cap, Jim. Maybe you can reach him with that!" He couldn't get at his own. It was all he and Jack could do to keep Jim anchored.

Jim seized his cap and, holding it by the peak, managed to stretch it far enough so that the exhausted squirrel could reach it.

"P-poor Hill B-billy—" Chuck sobbed, "I thought you were a goner that time!" He wiped the tears away with his sleeve.

When Hill Billy was back on his little master's shoulder, Jim squeezed the water out of his cap, then followed his father and the other boys to the cabin.

"The groundnut that we brought back looks like a good one, Dad." Jim motioned toward the eight tubers on the table. "Can we have them for supper?"

"Yes, I intended to fix them for supper if you brought any home. Chuck found some mushrooms this morning, too, so we'll have quite a variety of wild food to eat."

"I almost starved out there," Peter gestured in the general direction of the camp. "Think of all those things to eat in the woods and I didn't know about them. I'm going to study hard. I want to find food like the Indians did!"

The Ranger laughed. "I can see that Jack has been giving a lecture again." He dumped the groundnuts into the sink and began to scrub them. "Don't let me forget to put these in the oven about a quarter to four, Jim," he said.

"I'll remind you. Didn't Red and Tim intend to come in for lunch, Dad?" Jim asked as he dished up food for Jack, Peter and himself from the steaming kettles on the range.

"No, and, Son, I want you to take Star and the transceiver and ride up to Siskowit Bay and report after you get there. You'd better hurry, too! I thought you'd be back earlier," his father said.

"Siskowit Bay? Did the herd move again?" Jim asked as he hurriedly ate his food.

"Yes, last night," his father answered. Red and Tim decided that cowboy-style moose catching isn't so hot. They're going to build some box traps to use instead." He put the groundnuts in a pan, ready to pop into the oven. "I guess chasing the moose from Siskowit Bay clear over here would be too much of a good thing. Probably all break their necks—including the moose!"

"What do you mean, box trap?" Jim asked. "What are they?"

"A box trap," his father explained, "is a long box frame, built of poles over twice as long as a large moose. There are two trap doors, one on each end of the box. These doors are fastened to a catch in the center of the box." He paused to puff on his after-dinner pipe.

"Yes—then what?"

"Well, the catch in the center has a string attached which, in turn, is tied to some balsam branches or other moose feed. When the moose steps in the box to nibble at the food, he trips the catch and the doors at each end of the box drop shut."

"Golly, don't they ever try to get out?"

"I've never heard of one breaking out. Suppose they could if they knew what to do. They seem docile enough when they realize they can't get out."

"Humph! That's a lot simpler than chasing the critters up and down the trails." Jim asserted as he swallowed the last morsel of apple pie. "Boy, that was a good feed, Dad!

Guess I'll be going now. I'll call you as soon as I get there."

It was much later when Mr. St. Cyr consulted his watch again.

The big clock directly above the receiver gave the hours in Greenwich mean time. It was now 14:45 o'clock GMT and time for Jim to be calling.

Suddenly, as if Jim himself stood in the room, his voice broke the silence.

"Calling Forest Ranger station Isle Royale! How about it, Dad, do you hear me? Come in, please."

"Hello, Jim. You're coming through R-9 plus—clear as a bell. Over."

"I'm at Siskowit Bay. Red and Tim have finished the fifth trap and are baiting them all now. They plan to stay here overnight. I'm going to put their tent up for them and unpack their bed rolls. When they finish baiting the traps, they're going to start building a corral. They've decided that this is a better base to work from and it'll be easier for the boats to pick up the moose. The bay is plenty deep here."

"All right, Jim. Tell the boys we'll bring them up some provisions tomorrow. Have they grub with them for supper?"

"Yes. I'll be home in a couple of hours— I'm not so good at riding Star, but I'll make it. So long, Dad."

"Be careful. Don't take any chances on that rocky trail. Don't try to break any speed records. 'Bye."

The boys heard Jim laugh. "It wouldn't be a record I'd break. It'd probably be my neck! See you later. Signing off and clear with Isle Royale Ranger Station, WVV. This is portable WVV."

It was shortly after six when Jim arrived on Star. He yelled as he entered the clearing, "Come on out and help me off this walking rack of torture!"

His father ran to half-lift, half-drag him from the saddle. The boy limped beside his father up to the cabin. "I left the short-wave set with Red and Tim and showed them how to use it. They'll report on it at eight A.M. and 16 hundred. Jiminy! I hope I'm not this stiff tomorrow."

Roger laughed. "I can sympathize with you. I'm just getting back to normal myself! I can take the supplies up to them tomorrow, if you are too sore and stiff to go—and I know you *will* be!"

"I won't argue with you this time. But I intend to ride every day. Red said that if you do that, you get over being saddle-sore sooner. I hope he's right."

"I've heard that choice adage before, too, but never thought I'd have a chance to try it out myself. Supper's ready—everything you like, too."

Peter's initiation into the mysteries of forest vegetables proved a delight to him. The groundnut tubers had been baked to a delicious flakiness. Jack had split them and put a big pat of butter on each half, then popped them back into the oven to brown. The mushrooms had simmered in butter sauce and were a luscious tan.

While they were eating, Jim told how Red had chased a big cow moose and in its fright it had almost trampled him down. Then and there the two "moose hands" had decided on the box traps. When Jim left camp, Red and Tim were measuring out the corral and driving long stakes into the hard, trampled ground near the bank of the river.

They all ate in silence for a few minutes after Jim had finished his lively account.

Peter finally admitted, "I feel as if I were going to explode!" He rubbed his stomach. "I never tasted anything so good. And to think, it all grew in the woods."

"I never know when to stop eating when we have groundnut. Isn't it funny that more people living right in the woods and on farms, out in the country, don't even know there is such a thing." Jack pushed away from the practically empty table. "Can I talk to you for a minute, Jim?" he half-whispered to his brother.

"Sure, but why so mysterious?" Jim asked. "I don't see—"

Jack interrupted with a frown. "Quiet!" he motioned with his head. "In the bedroom."

He closed the door behind him and burst out, "I'm sort of bothered about Peter. From something he said this morning, I'm sure he'd like to know what's going to happen to him—and so would I. I was wondering if maybe we couldn't do something to help locate Duke. He might know something about Peter's relatives. You talk to lots of fellows up in Canada. He might have gone up there. After all, that's closer to Isle Royale than the States. Peter said Duke had mentioned Canada several times the last day he saw him. Could you kind of ask around when you talk to the fellows? You might accidently run onto something."

Jim shook his head doubtfully. "Might work—but it's only one chance in ten million that I'd ever talk to anyone who had seen him. Canada's an awfully big place, you know."

"I know that, but I think it's worth a try, anyway. What do you say—will you do it?"

"Of course I'll do it. What does this Duke look like?"

"Golly, Moses! I don't know, but I'll try to find out without telling Peter why. Then he won't be disappointed if we don't discover anything."

"Get as complete a description of him as you can. Even what his clothes looked like. I'll do what I can. But don't plan on anything happening because I don't." Jim knew the job would be like hunting a needle in a stack of moose moss.

11

Although Jim's muscles were stiff and sore, early the next morning he left the cabin on Star, with a large saddle bag full of supplies for Red and Tim. He took the shore trail and arrived just as they were sitting down by their campfire to eat breakfast. He could smell the pungent odor of coffee and sizzling bacon and fried potatoes before he could see the camp.

"Just in time," he called as he entered the clearing.

Red jumped up and came to meet him. "Bright and early must be your middle name. We didn't expect you till around noon."

"I started out early. I didn't know how fast I could go with these creaking muscles of mine."

Red chuckled. "How did you feel last night?"

Jim grimaced as he slid carefully from the saddle and then rolled his eyes and rubbed his legs. "Brother!" he groaned.

Red and Tim's laughter echoed against the rocks.

The men invited Jim to join them for a second break-fast. While they ate, they discussed the box traps.

Red said, "Those moose critters are sure foxy. They moved during the night and came down here. This is a good feeding ground. They've been here before because the ground is trampled hard at the edge of the woods, where they've browsed on the balsam boughs."

"Think you can get them with the box traps?" Jim asked.

"We'll see this morning. We baited eight traps last night with some young balsam shoots. If anything will get 'em, that will!"

"I hope you're right!"

"We started a corral up yonder. Found a natural spot. We can use the solid rock cliff where it juts out almost at a right angle to the water as one side and the water as the second side." Red took a long drink of hot coffee, smacked his lips and continued. "That way, we only have to build two sides of the corral. We finished one side last night, before we turned in. Should be able to get the front fixed this morning."

"Wish I could stay and help you, but I can't. Dad said you can keep the short-wave transmitter here. He's arranged with the department for a special license for you till your work is through. We'll listen for you on schedule each day, and you can let us know whenever you need supplies."

Jim was back at the cabin by noon.

Red and Tim stayed at the corral for some weeks, and either Jim or his father carried supplies to them regularly. One more week and it would be Thanksgiving.

The young St. Cyrs began to discuss how they'd cele-
brate the holiday when it was still ten days away, but
Jim didn't enter into the discussions. He grew morose
and glum.

Peter had readily fallen into the vigorous life of the
St. Cyrs and there were no longer hollows in his cheeks or
dark smudges under his eyes.

Jim liked having Peter around, but he spent more and
more time in the radio shack, while Jack and Chuck
taught their guest wood lore. Soon Peter could spot a
groundnut vine and mushrooms and many other products
of the soil as quickly as either Jack or Chuck.

It had taken many bits of conversation between the
boys for Jack to find out what Duke looked like. Jim kept
pressing him for new details, until the description finally
added up to this: age, about forty-five years; brown,
straight hair, graying at the temples; brown eyes, tanned
complexion. All this could have described many men in
Canada, of course.

There was only one mark by which Duke could instantly be identified. Over his left eye, almost at the hairline, was a two-inch scar. He had told Peter once that
he'd fallen from a hayrack when he was a boy and cut his
head.

Jim had given this word picture to all the Canadian
radio amateurs he'd talked to, but none had seen the
missing man until, quite late one night, Jim got his first
lead.

He was talking to VE4BQ, up in Manitoba—to a fellow
named Rufe that he'd played checkers with many times
over the air.

"How are you tonight, Jim? I've been camping on

your frequency for the last two days. I think I might have some news of that chap you were looking for. How are you receiving me?"

"Howdy, Rufe. You're coming through like a ton of bricks. There's no static tonight, so shoot. What have you got for me?"

"One of the Mounted Police was in the other night, and I mentioned to him about this guy you're looking for. He said that some man from the States had been reported sick over at one of the Indian camps. It seems that the Indians found him half-dead, out in the woods, and carried him back to their camp. The Mountie was on his way over to find out more about it."

"When will he be back your way?" Jim asked.

"He didn't say. But I asked him to let me know right away if it was the man with the scar. VE4BQ over to W9ZZO."

"I'll arrange a schedule with you for tomorrow night. Can you be on the air about seven-thirty? We'll be finished supper surely by then. W9ZZO over."

"That'll be fine with me, Jim. The work here at the trading post is a day and night job and I'm here all the time. I live in the back of the store. Over."

"I've read lots about the trading posts, but I never thought I'd be talking to the fellow that runs one. What do you trade?"

"Oh, we trade food and firearms and traps, just about everything you could name, for furs of all kinds and for cash. Ham radio has always been my hobby and it keeps me in touch with the world."

"It sure is a great hobby. I want Dad to let me go to college over in Houghton next summer and take a course in radio. I'm out of luck, though. He says I'm too young and he needs me here. Well, I'd better hit the hay. School in the morning, as usual. Hope you have some good news for me tomorrow night. So long. W9ZZO signing off and clear with VE4BQ. Good night, Rufe."

Jim yawned loudly as he put the transmitter to bed for the night. While he signed the logbook for the last time, he glanced carelessly over the entries. Since eight o'clock, he had talked to a "K" up in Alaska, a W1 up in Maine, four W6's out in California and Arizona, an XI in Mexico, two W8's in Ohio and the Canadian station. "It's a small world," he thought as he looked around at the QSL cards that papered the walls of his shack. For each card he'd received, he'd sent one in return, to confirm the radio contact and conversation.

Jim's father had left a light burning in the kitchen for him and it didn't take the weary boy long to crawl into bed.

Next morning, while his father was dressing, Jim related the facts Rufe had given him about the sick white man in the Indian camp in northern Canada.

The Ranger sat on the edge of his bed and listened closely. Finally he said, "Don't plan too much on this being Duke, Jim. Canada's a pretty big place, and a man could wander around up there for a long time without being spotted."

"Shall I say anything to Peter?" Jim asked.

"No! Don't breathe a word of this," Roger warned him quickly. "It's probably a false alarm. No use in getting all excited over nothing."

As soon as breakfast was over, the four boys got ready for school.

When they were crossing the top of the ridge, at the edge of the clearing, Jim dropped a little behind the others after saying to Jack, "Walk with me, I want to talk to you."

When his younger brother had dropped back beside him, he explained briefly the slight clue to Duke's whereabouts, then added, "Dad says for us not to mention it to Peter at all. It would break him up if it turned out to be a false alarm."

"Golly, I should say it would! Peter sure is getting to be a regular Indian in the woods. Every time we go out scouting, it's Peter that finds the darndest things to eat. The other day I found him reading up on botany."

"He's really a swell kid," Jim declared. "Seems like one of us now."

"I'd better catch up with him. He'll wonder what we're talking about and maybe smell a rat!" Jack hurried to join Chuck and Peter, while Jim kept himself company, striding along, hands in pockets, whistling a tune.

That night, Mr. St. Cyr made sure that supper was not delayed. As soon as the dishes had been done, Jim made a beeline for the radio shack.

It was one minute to seven-thirty when he turned on the transmitter and started the routine call.

"Calling Station VE4BQ, Manitoba, calling VE4BQ, calling VE4BQ. This is station W9ZZ0, Isle Royale calling and standing by. Come in, please."

Sharp bursts of static came from the loudspeaker when he turned up the volume so that he could hear without earphones.

"VE4BQ Manitoba, Trading Post number 42 calling W9ZZO, Isle Royale. You're coming through about R6 to 7, Jim. Weather brewing up here. By the sound of it, we're in for a ripsnorter! How are you receiving me? Come in please."

"W9ZZO back to Trading Post 42. You're coming in R8, Rufe old man! Heavy weather around us down here, too. Guess we can expect a little snow any time now. Well, now that we have disposed of the weather, what news do you have for me tonight?"

"Plenty! The Mountie got back here late this afternoon and he said that the white man at the Indian camp is very likely the man you're looking for. He talked with him, but couldn't get much out of him. He had his head all bandaged up so that the Mountie didn't see whether he had a scar on his forehead or not. The rest of the description fits him, though! The Mountie told him that you'd been looking for him and that Peter is staying with you. When he heard that, he closed his eyes and went to sleep. Wouldn't talk to the Mountie at all and wouldn't commit himself one way or the other as to whether he was Duke or not. He had a pretty bad siege of pneumonia and is too weak to talk much, I guess. We'll have to wait until he's stronger to get any word out of him. We'll keep an eye on him for you. He did say that he was going to stay at the camp with the Indians for a while and learn to trap. Guess that's about all the dope, Jim."

"You've done us a great favor tonight, Rufe. I hope that I can repay you in some way, sometime. I won't talk any longer now. Naturally, I'm anxious to get to my Dad and tell him the news. Will I see you tomorrow night?"

"No, I won't be on the air for four days. I have to go

in to town tomorrow. My wife will take care of the Trading Post until I return. I'll see you in four days, same time, same frequency."

"Fine business, Rufe! See you later then, and thanks again for your trouble. W9ZZO signing off and clear with VE4BQ. Good night!"

There were two stations on his frequency calling Jim, but the news was too good to keep to himself. He raced in to find his father.

12

Jim waited impatiently for his father while he tucked the three younger boys in bed. Then, while the Ranger banked the fires for the night, Jim poured out the story.

"Son," Roger put his hand gently on Jim's head, "I hope it is Duke. Perhaps he can tell us something about Peter's family. You've done more than your share toward finding him. I never realized what radio had done for you until you started on this man-hunt. I thought of it as only a hobby."

Jim spoke hesitantly, as though trying to keep his voice steady. "It's hard to explain just how I feel about radio, Dad. I believe if I had to give up puttering around with it, I just couldn't find anything else to take its place."

"Well, let's forget it for tonight. Tomorrow comes around early and supplies have to be taken to Red and Tim again. Star has certainly proved her worth to me since they came. I don't know how we'd have transported

141

supplies to them, unless we went by boat, and twenty miles by open boat in this cold weather isn't a very exciting prospect."

"*Brrr!* Don't mention it!" Jim faked a shiver as he started for his room.

Next morning, Jim helped his father pack supplies for the moose captors and rope them to the saddle. Star danced around, anxious to be off. She seemed to enjoy these trips.

As the boys were leaving the cabin for school, Mr. St. Cyr called to them. "I almost forgot to tell you to ask Miss Gene if she'd like to have Thanksgiving dinner with us tomorrow. I forgot to ask her yesterday when I saw her. No school now till Monday."

Jim inquired, "What time will I tell her we'll eat?"

"Well, tomorrow's a holiday, so I think we can eat about one o'clock. You boys can go to meet her, so she won't have to walk all the way alone. I'll get dinner."

"Okay, Dad. So long!" The boys called from the edge of the clearing.

Mr. St. Cyr made the trip to Siskiwit with food for Red and Tim in record time and he was home before the boys came from school. He had several Ranger reports to get ready for headquarters before the end of the week. He heard the boys when they entered the clearing and the rapid tattoo of their feet on the porch.

Jim's cap sailed across the room. "Hiya, Dad!" he called.

"Well," his father marveled, "you seem pleased as punch about something. What gives?"

Jim stood in the door, a smile stretching broadly from

ear to ear. "No school till Monday. We have Friday off, too. Dad—" he urged, "do you suppose we could go up to Siskiwit Friday, if Red and Tim are still there?"

His father considered this suggestion. Finally he said, "If they aren't through up there by then, yes! Oh, Red told me to send a radiogram to his wife. I almost forgot it! Good thing you spoke to me of Siskiwit or I might have slipped up entirely."

"How many moose have they trapped?"

"Red said the Coast Guard cutter took twenty off the island this morning. That makes eighty-four so far. Sixteen more before they're through. I don't think they'll get that many this afternoon."

"Did you ask them to come for dinner tomorrow?"

"Yes, but they didn't say for sure, whether or not they'd come. I'll know tonight when I talk to them. Did you invite Miss Gene?"

"I asked her, but she'd promised to go on a boat trip up around Rock Harbor with the Reed family. She said she was very sorry and hoped you'd ask her again."

"It's too bad I didn't think of it sooner. I've been so busy with these moose reports and all of my other work, that I didn't think about anything much else." He grinned at Jim, "But I sure will ask her again!"

Jim grinned back, then asked, "What time do you talk to Red and Tim again?"

"At six o'clock," his father answered. "Why?"

"If they aren't through by tonight, and as long as Miss Gene couldn't come, could we go up to the Big Siskiwit on Thanksgiving then—instead of Friday?"

"We'll wait and see what Red reports. If their job isn't done, I know they won't want to break things up and come down here for dinner." The Ranger ran his fingers through his hair. "It'd be a change. Maybe we can have an outdoor picnic. We can take our meat and get the rest of our food as we go along."

Chuck heard the last part of the conversation as he came in the cabin and started to hop around the room. "Whee—we're goin' on a picnic! We're goin' on a picnic!"

"Quiet, runt!" his father exclaimed, holding his ears to keep out the din, "Do you want to jar everything in the house? If you feel like hopping, hop outside!"

Jim went over to a window and looked out.

Peter sat on the porch, playing a few bars of a poignant refrain over and over again on his mouth-organ. Hill Billy had snuggled down in his lap for a nap. The sun, only an hour from the horizon, rested sharp, glittering fingers on the two figures.

Jim turned to his father. "That kid plays that song till it gives me the willies! If he'd only finish the darn tune, but over and over, it's the same few phrases."

Mr. St. Cyr shook his head at Jim. "Now! Now! Pipe down. Maybe he doesn't know the rest of it!"

Jim grunted, walked away from the window and threw himself into the chair in front of the big Ranger transmitter, with one leg draped over its arm. He turned the dials to the frequency of Red's short-wave walkie-talkie. It was exactly six o'clock and time for Red to report.

"Calling Ranger Station. This is Red. Can you hear me?" came blaring over the loudspeaker. Jim flipped a switch.

"We can hear you. Go ahead. What have you to report tonight?"

"Only got six moose this afternoon, so we don't break camp now. It'll be a day or so before we can leave."

"That's too bad, Red. As long as you can't get down here, how would you like company?" Jim laughed as he heard the younger boys slam the kitchen door and come to a halt in the doorway of the living room.

"Swell, who's coming?" Red answered.

"By the looks of the faces in the doorway here, I guess we'll all be there. Don't bother fixing anything for dinner. We'll bring it up."

"That's the best news I've heard in a long time. All Tim can cook is beans. So long. See you tomorrow."

"Good-by. We won't bring any beans! Ranger Station signing off and clear." Jim shut off the transmitter and looked at the shining young faces grouped in the doorway. He knew that the boys were tingling with excitement. Tomorrow they'd have a picnic at the corral! He wished he could feel the same way; instead, he felt weary and cheated. He slumped down in the chair, his foot nervously swinging back and forth.

13

vvvv • vvvv • vvvv • vvvv • vvvv • vvvv • vvvv

Thanksgiving morning dawned bright and crisp. With its sharp coolness mingled a tang of fir and pine.

Breakfast and the boys arrived at the table simultaneously.

Mr. St. Cyr said grace and then, for a few minutes, the clatter of knives and forks was all anyone could hear. The smell of hot griddle cakes, swimming in thick maple syrup, blended with the smoky fragrance of bacon and the sharp odor of coffee.

Jim was the first to speak. "What kind of meat are we taking with us, Dad?"

His father, fork lifted, answered, "What kind would you fellows like to take? This is your party."

"Can we take wieners and some steaks to broil over the campfire," Jim asked, "and, of course, some bacon strips for fish bait."

"Sounds perfect to me." The Ranger surveyed the other

146

interested young faces. "What do you fellows say? Does that sound good to you?"

"You bet! Swell! *Um-hummm!*" the chorus rang out.

"Steaks and wieners, it is then." He drained his cup. "We'll have to take coffee along too, and bread. There are plenty of good places to get water all along the way." Rising from the table, he said, "I'll get the meat ready and you boys clear up the table. Make it snappy because we want to get started right away. Jim, please get Star ready for the trip. She can carry the food in the saddle-bags, as we find it. We can all take turns riding her on the way home. I'm sure we'll be glad to have her with us before we get back tonight."

Jim nodded in agreement. "I was thinking that, too, Dad. The runts have never gone that far in one day before. I'd better take along some flashlights. It might be dark before we get back."

"Good idea!" his father agreed.

By the time the Ranger had finished cutting the steaks and packing the wieners, all the dishes were done and neatly arranged in the cupboard. Heavy coats were whisked out and gayly colored scarfs were hastily knotted around the boys' throats. Jim had saddled Star and carefully fastened to it the picnic basket, containing dishes, knives, forks and spoons, salt, pepper and matches.

Mr. St. Cyr stowed the meat, carefully wrapped, in a saddlebag, banked the fire in the kitchen stove so that there'd be no danger from sparks or spreading flames, then announced that they were ready to leave.

He headed the procession, leading Star by the bridle. Next came Jim, then Chuck, with Hill Billy, perched on his shoulder as usual, chattering away at his friends in the trees overhead. Peter and Jack brought up in the rear, Peter whistling snatches of the tune that lurked in the back of his mind.

As they walked over the trail winding through the narrow strip of land separating Siskiwit Lake from Siskiwit Bay, Hill Billy left Chuck's shoulder and bounded into the scrub along the trail every few minutes. He always bounded back with cheek pockets filled with hazelnuts from some low spot which the moose had not stripped.

As they went along, Jim pointed out various growths which he thought might interest Peter. On the west end of Siskiwit Lake, he showed him the differences between the varieties of white birch and the different age classes in the trees where fire had cut them down at various periods. Mr. St. Cyr seemed to be preoccupied with his own thoughts and had little to say.

After the group had passed the Little Siskiwit River, the rocky ground yielded to a richer earth. From the head of the procession, Roger called to the others, "Watch now for things for dinner. There'll be plenty of food to collect from here on."

"Wait a minute," Jack shouted from the back of the little column. "I found some young cattails."

"Cattails!" exclaimed Peter. "What is there to eat on a cattail?"

Mr. St. Cyr, who had handed Star's reins to Jim, walked back in time to hear the question. "We take the tiny spikes and roast them in the fire. After they're roasted, we peel the outer rind off and the white center is swell. In the spring, you can use the tender lower stem and root for salad, but now it's best roasted." He took a huge bunch of the cattails from Jim's outstretched hands and carried them back to the saddlebag.

At that instant, Peter dashed from the trail. "I see a bunch of groundnut vines! I'll be there in a second."

"That settles the potato question and one vegetable. Keep a sharp watch still, though. It's pretty late in the season to find much, but I think we may spot something more, if we look carefully."

Chuck was the next to call out. Hill Billy had scurried away to get a refill of hazelnuts, and Chuck had followed him. Directly off trail lay a damp, partly rotted log. On top of this flowered the soft white petals of a giant oyster mushroom fungi.

"Hey, Dad! I found a mushroom again. Is this kind good to eat?"

The Ranger hurried to his youngest son's side.

"Yes, this is especially good. See how snowy white they are. We can fry them in some of our steak fat." He glanced over the log and suddenly pointed to a bunch of green spikes growing at the far end. "There are some wild onions. Better take some along—for those that like them!"

"Haven't we almost enough stuff now?" Jim asked. He was anxious to get to the mouth of the Siskiwit. He wanted to be where the excitement was and this definitely was old stuff to him.

"Yes, I think we've almost all we'll need. I brought two big loaves of bread, in case we didn't find much along the way. With our steaks and wieners, onions, baked cattails, groundnut and fried mushrooms, what more could we want?"

"Oh, a nice big slice of pie!" Chuck smacked his lips.

"If I know you," his father replied as he tightened the

clamp on the bulging saddlebags, "by the time we get to the pie course, you'll be full to the eyebrows!"

A few minutes later, Chuck called out, "Say, Dad, I'm getting kind of tired. How much longer do we have to walk?" He rubbed his sturdy legs as he spoke.

"I'm surprised that you got this far without a lift." Mr. St. Cyr chuckled under his breath. "How about a nice little ride on Star's back?"

" 'Course I don't want you to think I'm a sissy, and I could walk the rest of the way, but I'd like to see how it feels to ride a horse."

"Help him up, Jim," the Ranger said.

Jim lifted the small boy into the saddle and turned his head quickly so that Chuck would not know he'd seen the expression of relief that flickered across his face before he could change it to extreme boredom. Obviously, it never would do to let his father know how tired he was. Why, he might not even let him go along next time!

"Well, will you look at his nibs! Riding Star as if he was glued there!" Jack couldn't resist teasing a little as he trudged along behind. "How does it feel to be a man of leisure?"

"Oh—" Chuck's answer sounded a trifle condescending, "er—very nice." Then he could hold his excitement in check no longer, "Golly! Is this the berries? But I'm up so high from the ground it looks farther down than it does up!"

"What a wonderful twist you give to the English language!" snorted Jim, "Miss Gene should hear you."

"Why bring that up? This is my vacation, so don't even talk about school!"

It was fifteen more minutes before the camp was

sighted and both Jack and Peter were beginning to grow
a little weary, too. Jim had traveled the trails often and
was used to the up and down walking. Nevertheless, the
sight of the camp and the ring of an ax quickened their
pace until they were within shouting distance.

Red was near the corral, pounding in a few extra stakes,
to strengthen the walls against the scratching of insect-
irritated moose. Here they could not submerge in the
water that formed one side of their pen. The unsure foot-
ing and treacherous rocks prevented this. So, to rid themselves of the flies and ticks that tormented them, they
rubbed against the poles and stakes which enclosed them.

Tim was stirring up the campfire. A huge tripod, such
as the Indians have used for centuries, straddled the
blaze. A kettle swung from a chain dangling in the center.
The spicy odor of burning tamarack and pine dulled the
heavy, offensive smell of moose.

"Hi, Tim!" screamed Chuck from his perch, and waved
so violently that Hill Billy was almost thrown from his
shoulder. "Golly, it's sure a long way down here, but we
made it!"

"So you did. Hi, fellas! We were beginning to wonder
if we were going to have company for dinner or whether
we had better start cooking our own. I was goin' to open
a can of beans!" Tim winked at the Ranger.

Red loped up in time to hear the end of the conversa-
tion. "Thank heavens you got here! Another meal of
Tim's beans and I wouldn't have the strength to walk to
the corral. I sure hope you brought some chow with you."
Red was eyeing the stuffed saddlebags with frank interest.
"And not beans either!"

"That saddlebag is chock-full of good things to eat," the

Ranger told him, "things I'll bet you never heard of before
—and probably never will again, after you leave the island."

"How come?"

"We're having our wild food menu today. Ever eat
roast cattails or oyster mushrooms or wild onions?" Jim
teased.

"Can't say I have. Don't tell me you eat fuzzy cattails!"

The boys laughed heartily at Red's howl of dismay.
"No, we don't eat the fuzzy part, only the root and stem
of a young spike!" Jim answered.

"Howling cats! Do you mean we're goin' to have that
for dinner?" Red turned sadly to Tim. "You win. Open
up a can of those refugees from an army kitchen! Cattails! Ugh!"

"No beans today. You're going to eat cattails and ask
for more, or my name isn't Roger St. Cyr."

"I'm waiting to be convinced, but I know right now I
won't like them."

"Don't be too sure of yourself. You're going to feel kind
of foolish when you say 'Yum yum' and ask for more.
Help me with this grub, Jim. Jack, you and Peter can
clean the groundnuts down on the beach. Hurry now, we
want to get this stuff in these hot coals."

Jack and Peter carried the tubers down to the lake and,
with the aid of handfuls of coarse sand, rubbed the
groundnuts until no trace of earth clung to the skins. "I
wish we had thought of bringing some fishhooks," Jack
observed out loud as he looked out over the sun-drenched
water.

"I was afraid you'd try to fish with a pin again," Peter

teased, "so I stuck some hooks and line in my coat pocket."

"Here!" He handed Jack the hooks and small ball of fish line. "Let's hustle these nuts and then see if we can catch some fish."

They raced back with their cleaned groundnuts and helped Mr. St. Cyr put them in the bed of coals. The cattails had already been covered and were sizzling and steaming in their deep nest.

"Can we go fishing off the rocks, Dad? Peter brought some hooks along. Can we?" Jack persisted.

"I think I can manage the rest of this, all right. But if by any chance you get some fish, clean them before you bring them back here. I'll call you when dinner's ready."

Jim hadn't said a word during this time. Now he scooped up a big bunch of the spicy green stems, "I'll clean the onions, Dad, down at the lake. Be right back." As he walked to the beach, he could see Tim, with a wide grin on his homely face, listening to Red grumble.

"Groundnuts! Leeks! Cattails! Good thing you brought some decent meat. I'll have something civilized to eat. Cattails! Thanksgiving feast. *Phooey!*"

Mr. St. Cyr evidently heard this explosion, too, because Jim heard him retort, "I can hear you sing a different tune pretty soon. You just wait and see!" The Ranger tried hard to keep a straight face, as he measured out coffee and added it to the kettleful of boiling water hanging above the fire. "Bring that basket over, will you, the one that's lashed to the saddle! It has our meat spit and wiener sticks in it and the rest of the things we'll need."

Red walked off, mumbling to himself, and Jim hurried

to the lake to clean the onions. The voices of the men still carried to him on the crisp air.

"If this tastes anything like the meals you rustled up at the cabin—" Tim said hopefully.

"Even better," the Ranger interrupted him. "Of course, the names are strange, but the food they represent can't be beat!"

"I'll take your word for it!" Tim pointed to the handmade table in front of their tent. "Shall I bring this over near the fire?"

"I think you'd better. It'll be handy for me to dish out things on, buffet style."

Jack and Peter, with strips of raw bacon for bait, walked along the beach and finally found a rock projecting far enough out so that from it they could reach deep water with their lines. The pair scrambled up on top of the rock and threw their lines out as far as they would go. Jim watched them as they sat there quietly.

Suddenly Peter jerked his arm. He yelled, "I've got one! I've got one!" and jumped to his feet. He had to pull the fish in fast, as he had no pole and reel to play it with. When he finally got it up on the rock it turned out to be a big, yellow-bellied perch, with great, glassy eyes! It flopped around until Peter could get up enough courage to grab it and take the hook from its mouth. Jim chuckled as he watched the changing expressions flit across the boy's face.

"That's sure a dandy. Now all you have to do is clean it," he heard Jack say. Jim knew that Jack didn't care whether he caught any fish or not, because the cleaning ordeal always repulsed him. Still, it was a family rule that any fish good enough to keep must be cleaned immediately. Mr. St. Cyr had made the rule several years before, after the boys returned from a fishing spree with a big basketful of uncleaned fish. By the time they'd walked back to the cabin, the fish were dry and stiff.

Peter climbed down from the rocky perch and proceeded to clean the fish at the water's edge. He laughed as he saw Jack start to pull in his line. "Get one?" he called.

"I guess so. I shouldn't have laughed at you so quick."

"Misery loves company. Come on down, the weather's fine."

Jack descended with his wiggling catch, a perch similar to Peter's and squatted down beside his friend. "These'll be good cooked over the fire," he said with growing cheerfulness, as he cut the head off with one quick stroke. "Fish have a different taste outdoors. Guess maybe it's the smoky taste they get from the wood."

"There mine's all cleaned. I think I'll try for another." Peter jumped back up to his perch on the rock and threw his line in the water again.

"He's a persistent lad," Jim thought as Peter caught two more fish. Jack caught one more before his father called the boys to dinner. They raced over the uneven, rocky ground with their catch and plopped them down on a flat stone near the fire.

"Aren't they beauties?" cried Peter.

"They certainly are. But now let's eat," Mr. St. Cyr said. "I'm starved, and I know the rest of you must be, too. Everything's on the table, so just dig in. Chuck got a head start on you, as usual." He beckoned to Red. "I'll fix up your plate for you, and I'll bet you ask for more."

Red's mouth began to water as he watched the Ranger

heap up his plate. First a steak, topped with mushrooms and gravy, then a groundnut with its golden crown, then a generous serving of cattail "asparagus," baked and black, and a couple of onions. He handed the full plate to Red, saying, "The bread is all buttered and waiting and the coffee is poured. Eat hearty!"

By this time, Red's disbelief had turned into a hungry, gnawing, empty feeling in the pit of his stomach and he eyed his rations eagerly.

"If I didn't know what this stuff was, I'd think I was back home. It sure looks good—better than it sounded when you told me about it."

Mr. St. Cyr helped each one in turn to the meat and soon, everyone had a heaped plate before him. For a few minutes they were all much too busy to talk. Red finally broke the silence. "I'll have to apologize to you, Roger, for the way I talked. This is one of the best meals I've ever eaten. No foolin'! I didn't think you had all your buttons when you brought this stuff into camp. But I should have known better. You Ranger fellows know the woods, all right. I'll never doubt your word again."

Roger St. Cyr laughed. "That's our business. We have to know these things, so that we're never without some kind of food. But remember, we have the Indians to thank for the know-how."

Jim groaned. "I'm so full, I don't want to hear the word food for a week! What I need is a walk. I'm going down to the corral." He put his plate on the table and got up.

14

wwv • wwv • wwv • wwv • wwv • wwv • wwv

As Jim walked slowly away from the lit-
tle group, he heard Red declare "I ate too much, and here
I had thoughts of a dinner of beans again."

Mr. St. Cyr scraped a plate of scraps into the fire, then
asked, "Think you'll be through tomorrow?"

"The boat is supposed to come in for the last load tomorrow noon. That finishes up our work here, and I can't
say that I'll be sorry. It smells too much like winter for
me, and, besides, I'll be glad to get back home." Red
gazed out over the bay. "It's been nice up here, and we've
enjoyed meeting you and the kids." He turned to Tim.
"Haven't we?"

"Sure have. It's been an experience, too. Now I can
tell my grandchildren about the time I went hunting
moose, and look them straight in the eye."

Red laughed. "That's more than you can do when you
tell them some of your other stories!"

Just as Jim was getting close to the corral, the three

younger boys caught up with him. They all stood looking through the wide bars at the great, ungainly animals. Red and Tim had thrown in a lot of balsam boughs and hazelnut underbrush. A large pile of ground hemlock lay in one corner of the corral. An immense cow on the far side of the pen was kneeling on her two front legs, chewing the bark from a young mountain ash.

Peter spoke over his shoulder to Jim. "They're really funny creatures, aren't they? See how they carry their heads, straight out, as if to balance those big antlers. How can they get through a forest trail with such big horns?"

"That's always been a mystery to me, too," Jim remarked as he absent-mindedly peeled the bark off the logs in front of him. "But a moose has terrific speed in the woods." He smiled. "His huge donkey-ears certainly don't make him a beauty winner, but they can even hear a flea sneeze!"

They all laughed.

"Why is that cow kneeling down over there, eating?" Chuck asked, indicating the cow chewing the bark from the mountain ash.

"Well," explained Jim, "their front legs are longer than the hind legs. They're built that way so that, when they wade around in the bog lakes, they don't sink down too far. That makes their heads much higher than their hind quarters and, besides, their necks are short, so when they stand on a level place, they can't reach the ground very well with their mouths. I guess it's just a matter of comfort for them to eat that way."

"Golly!" Chuck puckered his mouth to whistle, but only a hissing sound came from between his lips. "She looks like she's saying her prayers!"

The boys hooted at this. "Whoever heard of a moose saying her prayers?" Jim teased.

"She looks like it, anyway!" Chuck began to climb up the logs in the fence.

Jim warned, "Be careful up there. You might fall!"

"I'm all right," Chuck retorted as he balanced on the top rail.

Then it happened.

A big cow moose, scratching herself on one of the upright poles farther along the same side of the fence, shook the entire top rail.

Chuck wasn't expecting the sudden jerk, and over he flew, right into a heap of balsam boughs inside the corral, almost under the shaggy black nose of a startled cow!

Jack yelled, "Dad! Quick!" then stood so helpless with fear that he couldn't move. Peter gasped once, and could only stare in terror as the big cow moose inched nearer to investigate this man-calf who sat on her dinner!

The second Chuck started to fall, Jim had reached for him and had missed grabbing his jacket by only a hair. When Chuck landed in the balsam, Jim took a running jump and vaulted the fence. He caught his small brother almost as soon as he landed and quickly stood him on his feet.

"Run!" he snapped. "I'll be right behind you." Jim snatched a big bough from the side of the pile and held it out in front of him as he backed up.

It afforded no real protection, but served to distract the cow until Chuck could climb the fence. The moose was snorting now and moving closer, her big, black quivering nose almost touching the tips of the long branch. The rest of the moose were closing in, too. Perspiration beaded Jim's forehead. He'd seen carcasses that had been trampled by angered moose—cut to ribbons by the sharp hoofs.

By this time the three men had sprinted to the fence and were leaping over. Suddenly, Jim felt a shoulder next to his, and a long, hot stick from the campfire was thrust forward in a strong hand.

"Hurry!" His father stepped in front of him. "No telling what they'll do next!" He stuck the hot brand in the leading moose's face, and she backed up in surprise, snorting a little and shaking her head.

While the huge cow stood, apparently deciding what to do, Jim and his father clambered over the fence and dropped to the ground on the other side.

"Fast thinking, lad." Tim spoke quietly as Jim and his father stood wiping their faces. "Those critters are pretty restless since they've been corralled, and you never know just what they'll do when they're surprised like that."

Chuck rushed up and wound his arms around his father's leg. "Golly, Dad, I'm sorry I fell in, but that doggone ol' moose gave the fence a push and I slipped."

"You're a lucky little boy, do you know that?" The Ranger's face was stern. "If Jim hadn't gone in after you when he did, I'd hate to think what you'd look like now." He strode over to where Jim sat on a fallen log.

His hand on the boy's shoulder, he said, "That was a brave thing for you to do, Son!"

The color was flowing back into Jim's pale face. He smiled up at his father. "Aw shucks, skip it! 'Twasn't anything. You were the one that really stopped her."

His father squeezed his shoulder a bit, then turned

quickly and walked away. He didn't want any of them to see that his eyes suddenly were wet with tears.

Back at the fire, he poked at the embers and put on another log. By the time the rest joined him, he was his usual controlled self.

"I think we'd better start back," he announced. "We've a long trip to take and I'm afraid we won't make it before dark. Let's load up." He seized the saddlebag, which he'd packed right after dinner, and went over to saddle Star.

"I wish we were going to stay all night," Jack said wistfully, as he scuffed his toe in the hard dirt. "You don't suppose Dad'd let us stay, do you?" He looked hopefully at Jim.

"Nix! He'd have white hair by tomorrow if you stayed. One near-accident is enough for one day. Next time we might not be so lucky!" Jim rose from the log and pulled down his jacket.

"Well, I wondered, that's all!"

"Forget it, runt, and start packing your junk."

Evidently Chuck was none the worse for his experience in the moose pen. While Jim helped his father pack Star, he ran around the edge of the clearing, trying to locate some hazelnut scrub. It had been pretty well browsed by the moose herd before Red and Tim had arrived, so the boy couldn't find any nuts for Hill Billy. "You're not very hungry, if you won't even go looking for your own food, you lazy thing! There isn't anything here, so you'll have to wait till we get home."

Hill Billy cocked his head on one side and scolded. He wasn't worrying about food. His cheeks were puffed out twice their size with pine cone tidbits he'd gathered while the rest of them had been eating dinner. He flicked his saucy tail in Chuck's ear, then sat bracing himself with it.

At last Star was saddled and ready to go.

"All set, let's go!" Mr. St. Cyr started out at the head of the little band again, leading the mare.

The three younger boys scampered along next, first on one side of the trail and then on the other, while Jim brought up the rear. The sun was glowing big and red in the western sky and birds flew up from the dust of the path, where they had been sunning themselves. Now and then the pungent smell of a rotting fir tree clung near the path they followed.

Chuck was the first one to wilt. They had walked about five miles when, he stopped in his tracks and begged, "Do you s'pose Star could carry me again, Dad? Golly, I'm tired!" His face puckered up in a little boy scowl.

"Whoa, Star! You have a passenger." The Ranger lifted the weary child to the saddle. "You've done well to walk as far as you have today, Son. I'm sure Star won't even notice the difference with you on her back."

Jack and Peter were plodding quietly along in the trail now—not so many side trips to investigate some colorful bush or tree. Jim chuckled to himself as he noticed them sticking closer to the path. A hush was settling down over the forest. The furred and feathered creatures were preparing for darkness.

Another mile, and Jack began to lag, with Peter dragging at his heels. After a while, Mr. St. Cyr stopped the mare.

"I don't think Star would mind a couple more passengers. What do you say? Want a lift?"

"Do we want a lift!" yipped both boys in unison. "I can

hardly pick up my feet, I'm so tired," groaned Jack. Peter accepted the invitation without any comment.

Jim teased the trio of riders as they moved forward. "Talk about a bunch of sissies—you three make a nice picture up there!"

"Humph!" snorted Jack. "My dogs were barking some! How're you coming?" He turned his head slightly so that he could look over his shoulder at Peter, who was sitting with one arm around Jack's middle, to help him keep his seat.

"Fine, but it's kind of slippery back here. If I don't hang on to you, I'm afraid I'll fall off the rear." He rolled his eyes as he added, "But I sure am glad for the lift!"

Jim walked at the horse's side, to keep an eye on the boys. "How about a little music as we walk, Peter?" he asked.

Instantly, Peter dug in his pocket with his free hand and pulled out his mouth-organ.

They sang school songs first, then drifted into old favorites and finally began to clown. Mr. St. Cyr started it when he suggested that they sing, "Tramp, Tramp, Tramp, the boys aren't marching!" From then on, they parodied the songs, howling with laughter at their own silly words.

Blackness settled over the forest and before they realized it, they were advancing in the gloom of night.

"Have you your flashlight handy, Jim?" Mr. St. Cyr asked.

"Yes, and yours is in the outside pocket of the saddle-bag—stick your hand inside and you'll find it."

They had passed the end of Siskiwit Lake. Their lights cast eerie shadows on the bushes that walled some parts of the trail and made huge, grotesque figures leap with long legs each time they took a step. The *whoo—whoo* of the night owl from its perch near the trail sent shivers coursing up and down the backs of the three boys riding Star. The maniacal laughter of the loon from the nearby lake made them wish they were home, sitting in front of their cozy fire.

To Jim and his father, this was only a familiar night noise, without which the trip would have seemed unreal.

Apparently Peter was uneasy, for he began to play the rhythmic bit of a tune that seemed always to linger beyond reach in a pocket of his mind.

Jim listened to the boy for a few minutes, as he tried to pick out the rest of the tune. "Where did you ever hear that melody?" he asked finally.

"I don't know. It keeps popping into my head whenever I play or whistle and it sounds familiar to me, but I never can finish it. I like it, don't you?"

"Yes, it has a refrain that keeps repeating itself. Sounds like a lullaby to me. Don't you remember where you heard it?"

"No, but it must have been long ago, when I was a very little boy. I used to sing it just before I went to bed, when I was at the orphanage. The Sisters always let me sing it for a prayer. I used to want them to sing it with me, but none of them ever did. They said they didn't know it."

"That's strange." Exciting thoughts began to form in Jim's mind but he didn't mention them to Peter. It seemed so implausible. What could a song possibly mean to a small boy in an orphanage? Best to forget the notion entirely. But the idea wouldn't leave him. It persisted in nagging at one corner of his brain.

When the travelers neared the cabin clearing, they could hear the night plaint of the whippoorwill rise and fall over the ridges. The last song of the giant bullfrog echoed from the marshy hollows. It was as if each forest creature was saying good-by to a beautiful summer and fall. The smell of frost hovered low.

The cabin stood out, solid and clear in the moonlight. It was a haven of rest tonight.

Mr. St. Cyr helped the tired children from their high perch and the three of them, Jack in the lead, dragging their feet, entered the cabin and lighted the lamps.

Jim took Star into the makeshift stall and rubbed her down for the night.

"Perfect day, eh, Jim?" his father asked as he threw food in the manger for Star.

"Sure was. But I'm bushed! It must be around ten o'clock, by the looks of the moon. My watch stopped a while ago, and I didn't bother to set it."

The Ranger looked at his watch. "Yes, it's exactly twelve minutes past ten. Not a bad guess."

As the pair walked toward the cabin, Jim drew a deep breath and said, "That moon's a cold one. Bet we have snow tonight."

"I won't bet with you, because that's my guess, too."

At the foot of the porch steps, Mr. St. Cyr paused and put his hand on Jim's arm. "Did you hear any more from that fellow up in Canada?"

"Nope. I have a schedule with him in the morning. He'll be back from his trip by then. If it is Duke, what shall I have them do?"

"Make sure first that it is. All we want of him is a little information about Peter. I haven't had a chance to tell you before, but I got a very sketchy report from the mainland yesterday. The authorities checked both the orphanage records and neighbors who knew Peter's adopted parents and all they can find out is that he was taken to the orphanage when his parents were killed. His older sister went West. So far they've been unable to locate her."

"But what about the neighbors at the farm?" Jim asked.

"All any of them seem to know is that he was an adopted boy. It seems the old couple were close-mouthed," Mr. St. Cyr said.

"Do you have to go out tomorrow?" Jim asked.

"No, I'm staying home. I must keep in touch with the Coast Guard cutter and with Red and Tim. This is their last trip, and we don't want any slipup. Of course, they are anxious to get out of here before the freeze-up." Mr. St. Cyr stood tamping tobacco in his pipe for a last smoke before bed.

"In that case, I can let you know what I find out. Better yet, why don't you come out to the shack with me, and talk to the fellow yourself?" Jim suggested, in the hope that somehow he could change his father's mind about radio school through this direct association.

"What time is your schedule?" the Ranger asked warily.

"At eight-thirty."

"I'll come. Now, to bed with you."

" 'Nite, Dad."

"Good night, Son—and thank you."

15

〰 • 〰 • 〰 • 〰 • 〰 • 〰 • 〰

Jim woke in the morning to hear tiny, icy pellets dancing against the panes. They bounced to the ledges and rolled to the ground. Each window wore a new white curtain of frost in fern patterns.

Mr. St. Cyr had heaped the fireplace in the boy's room with logs, so that when they jumped out of bed, the place would be toasty and warm. He followed Jim out to the radio shack and shivered until the boy had the old-fashioned buck stove roaring.

At eight-thirty on the dot, Jim proceeded to call Manitoba.

"Calling VE4BQ, calling VE4BQ. This is W9ZZO Isle Royale calling and standing by. Come in, Rufe."

"VE4BQ Manitoba coming back to W9ZZO, Isle Royale. Hello, Jim ol' man. Sounds good to hear your voice again. Got back late last night. Was afraid I wasn't going to make it, though. We're having a heck of a blizzard up here. About three feet of snow dropped on us in two

167

days. At that rate, it won't be long before we're snowed under. How are you receiving me? Manitoba standing by."

"Isle Royale—W9ZZO back to VE4BQ. You're coming through fine business. Dad is out here in the shack with me. He wants to talk to you." Jim handed the microphone to his father, who was standing by the stove, thawing out.

"Hello, Rufe." Mr. St. Cyr said. "Heard any more from the Mounted Police about the sick man at the Indian camp? If so, shoot!"

"Yes, the Mountie was here last night when I got back. He had gone to the camp. Said that the man there has no scar on his forehead. He talked freely to the Mountie, and it seems that he's some drifter that thought he could hunt and trap up here and make a stake overnight. He's getting better, though, and the description Jim gave me fits him, but no forehead scar and wrong name. Break."

"Doggone it, anyway. I hoped we had something there. Well, thanks a lot for your trouble. Over."

"Sorry I can't help you. Could I speak to Jim again?" There was a slight pause while Jim and his father changed places. . . . "When will I see you again, pal?"

"I'll be on tomorrow. Can't say what time, though. I'll be on this same frequency, so listen for me when you get on. Thanks again for your trouble. See you later. W9ZZO signing off and clear with VE4BQ."

Jim and his father walked back to the cabin without speaking. Their feet made crunchy sounds in the white carpet of snow.

Jack and Peter had breakfast ready and in five minutes they were all sitting down, eating.

Presently Mr. St. Cyr asked, "Peter, when you left Ohio with Duke, where did you go?"

Jim wondered what his father was getting at.

Peter swallowed a bit of toast, then answered straightforwardly. "First we went to Detroit. Duke thought he might get a job in a factory, but after we got there, he didn't like the city—said it was too big and noisy, after living on a farm for so long. I was afraid, too—I was glad he left." He absent-mindedly took another bite of toast and a faraway look came into his eyes.

"Yes," the Ranger's quiet voice encouraged him, "then what?"

"Then we went to a little town called Frankfort. Duke worked for a while on the car ferries that leave from there. When the tourists started to come, it got too crowded for him."

Mr. St. Cyr frowned slightly. "Where did you go then, Peter?" he asked.

"Oh, we went across the Lake to Menominee; then up to Escanaba, just in time to get in on the smelt run; and then up to the copper country. Duke wanted to get work in the mines."

"Did he?" Mr. St. Cyr prodded quietly and Jim forgot to eat.

"They weren't hiring anyone then. They said ore wasn't moving very fast, and some of the mines were shut down. He sure was sore. Then he heard about this island from someone and wanted to come here to fish."

"Yes—"

"And everything was swell," Peter's voice quavered, "till—till he fell in that hole—"

"Pit, you mean," the Ranger corrected him.

"It looked like a hole to me then. And you know what happened after that as well as I do."

"Yes, I guess we do—although I hope it isn't the end of the story."

It was later in the day that Jim noticed his father's preoccupied stare as he sat in front of the Ranger transmitter. Jim had just come in from the radio shack.

"What's up, Dad? You look as if you'd lost your last friend. What's eating you?"

"Nothing definite," his father answered after a moment. "Tell you later. The Coast Guard cutter should be here soon. Why don't you boys watch for it from the pier?"

"Good idea." Jim nodded. Evidently his father wanted to be alone for a few minutes. Probably the news he'd received from the mainland wasn't so good!

The boys could see the smoke of the cutter in the distance as they ran out on the pier. The water looked dark and cold and stormy. The ship was nosing steadily into the white breakers with her heavy load, riding low and solid.

Red and Tim were standing at the railing as the cutter edged close to the pier to tie up. Huge, thick ropes were tossed down to the eager hands of the youngsters, hopping around below.

"Make her fast, boys! This is a pretty strong wind for these critters. Don't reckon they like it much either, from all the bawlin' an' fussin' they've been doin'!" Red wiped the cold spray from his face.

"Don't know's I like it much muself!" drawled Tim. He did look kind of green around the gills and the boys giggled as he made his way unsteadily down the gangplank to the dock.

"Can't stay but long enough to send out a couple of messages to the mainland," Red told Jim as they hurried up to the cabin. "What an end to our stay here—an up and down ride with a bunch of seasick moose!" he chuckled.

"You can laugh," Tim prophesied darkly as he staggered along beside Red, his green complexion unfaded, "but don't forget, we've got a nice, long ride ahead of us yet and I'll bet my hat you're gonna feel sky-blue-pink inside before we get there."

"I won't bet on it; you're too likely to win," Red replied.

Mr. St. Cyr was talking to Houghton when Jim, the cowboys and the three youngsters came into the cabin. It was a couple of minutes before he finished with his report.

"Stand by Houghton. The cutter is tied up at the pier now. Here's Red and Tim. I'll let you talk to them." He handed the mike to Red, who stood behind him waiting.

"Hello, Houghton," Red's voice drawled. "We're on our way over with the last load. Pretty rough going, too. Don't know what time we'll get in. But for the love of Pete, get the cars ready to take the moose off. They're a sick bunch!"

The operator at Houghton laughed. "We'll be waiting at the dock for you, Red. Any messages for your family?"

"Yeah, tell them we're taking the first train out of Houghton for God's country! Too much cold and snow here for me." He made his teeth chatter. "Be seein' you late this afternoon." He handed the microphone back to Mr. St. Cyr, who said, "Guess that's all for now, Houghton. I'll be back on again at six o'clock. Have some paper handy. I'll have a big order for you then. Isle Royale off and clear. So long."

"Righto, see you later. Houghton clear."

The Ranger switched off the transmitter and turned in his chair. "So you've got a sick bunch with you? Too bad you couldn't have made the trip yesterday, when it was calm. This lake is bad stuff in a storm."

"Right. The quicker we get those critters on dry land, the better I'll like it."

A short time later, Jim, his father and the younger boys stood on the pier, watching the Coast Guard cutter head out due south, bound for Houghton and the train which would transport their bawling herd to the Cusino Game Refuge.

During supper that night, the boys did little talking and Mr. St. Cyr none at all. At the end of the meal, the latter retired to his seat before the transmitter and lost himself in a deep haze of pipe smoke as he called in the long list of supplies he needed to the mainland.

When the dishes were cleared away, Jim threw himself down in front of the fireplace with a radio textbook and tried to study. Jack got out his whittling set and began to work on the tiny boat he'd started a long time back. Chuck crawled into bed, worn out with the day's adventures. Peter stretched out beside Jim and played his mouth-organ softly, always ending the second or third tune with seven bars of his lullaby.

The pages of the radio textbook blurred before Jim's eyes. Wonder what the fellows are doing, he thought. Can't get my mind on studying tonight; might just as well go out to the shack and see what's going on. He tossed the book aside, pushed himself to his feet and stretched.

"What's the matter?" Jack asked, looking up for a moment from his whittling.

"Nothing. Guess I'll go on the air for a while."

"Oh!" Jack was no longer interested. The wooden boat had begun to take shape in his hands and the notes of the lullaby enclosed the room with its soft, embracing strain.

Jim, bundled up warmly, interrupted his father's reverie.

"If you want me, I'll be in the shack," he said.

Mr. St. Cyr nodded. "Give the fellows my regards."

"Yeah." Jim turned and walked slowly from the cozy room. He hesitated on the porch. The sound of breakers hitting the rocky coast mingled with the weird call of the loon. The sharp, coughing bark of a wolf set up a protesting reply from the screech owl and, in the distance, the call of a yearling moose mingled with the sound of the wind.

Jim leaned against the railing and looked out over Superior. The moon was high. It cast a path of light across the turbulent waters, straight toward him. The wind had freshened since afternoon. He breathed deep, long breaths. Yes, there was something in the air, something that spelled trouble. He couldn't name it, but he could detect it.

He hurried to the ham shack. Sharp gusts of wind hit him, and he bent forward to partially escape its force.

The shack was cold. He pushed the door shut and leaned against it. Might as well build a fire, he thought. It's too chilly to sit in here this way.

He threw kindling into the little buck stove and then

a lighted match. There was a puff of smoke as the kindling ignited and the fire roared mightily for a few minutes before he threw a wood chunk on the hot coals. It sparked and snapped like tiny firecrackers.

Turning on all the filaments, first the transmitter, then the receiver and the VFO took but a moment. He threw the antenna double-pole, double-throw switch from the ground side to the antenna side and tuned the receiver slowly from 7200 to 7300, the phone portion of the forty meter band. Not many CQ's coming through, he thought. Guess I'll go on 75 meters. Maybe I can talk to Katchy.

The band was alive with signals tonight, but lots of QRN. Must be a storm brewing. He retuned the transmitter, after replacing the 40 meter coils with 75 meter coils, from the shelf over the transmitter.

On 3900 he could hear Tex, W8MAZ, in Detroit, in QSO with a Canadian across the river, in Windsor. They were discussing antennas. Jim tuned a few KC's. About 3910, a traffic net was in session. He listened for a time. Messages from all over the globe were being passed along, some for delivery, some for QSP (relay). On 3920, he found Katchy, Jerry and Tom, all busy taking turns ribbing each other. He tuned the VFO to 3920 and retuned the transmitter slightly for maximum output. As Jerry turned it over to Tom for a transmission, Jim broke in.

"Break! Break!" He flipped switches again and thought as he did it, "I'm going to install that relay one of these days, so I'll have only one switch to throw.

"Sounds like 'his nibs,'" Tom laughed. "How about it—shall we talk to him?"

Jerry broke fast. "We might as well. He'll QRM us till we let him in, anyway. Hi, Jim, how's tricks?"

Jim smiled as he broke back. "I didn't hear anything worth while going on, so thought I'd give you guys a good signal to listen to for a change. Over."

Katchy broke in order. "Never mind, Jim. We feel sorry for you, so we'll talk to you." His chuckle was infectious. "Say, by the way, Jerry, we're sitting here in Duluth, waiting for clearance. We'll be loaded in an hour or so. How does the weather look?"

"Last weather report says, storm on way down from Canada. Is your skipper shoving off, anyway?"

"Yeah. We're ready whenever we get clearance. The skipper is a crusty ol' salt. A storm is right in his mitt! W8XI/Marine Mobile to W9XXM, with W9ZZO and W9ZZY in the hole."

"You can have him, I don't want him. I'm sure glad I'm not out on Superior tonight. I've got to sign now, too. Company just dropped in. See you guys tomorrow. Got your water wings, Katch? 73. W9ZZM, Houghton, off and clear. Take it, Jim."

"This is W9ZZO, Isle Royale. Roger. S'long, Tom, see you later. Say, Katchy, it's sure blowing up a gale over here. That wind's a nor-easter! Better tell your skipper to stay in port. How about it, Jerry?"

"W9ZZY, Devil's Island. Yeah. I gave them the weather earlier on 51. Most of the ships are sticking close to port or shelter to ride this one out. Better tell him, Katchy. It's brewing up a nasty one. Over."

"W8XI/Marine Mobile returning. The day I tell the skipper what to do—boys—*that* will be the day!" Katchy changed the subject then. Obviously he was worried because Jim could detect an undertone of concern in his small talk.

The trio kept up the banter until almost 10:30 and then Katchy broke it up.

"Gotta secure, fellows," he explained, "we'll be leaving soon, so see you tomorrow. Sure has been a swell Q-so. 73 and take 'er easy. W8XI/Marine Mobile at Duluth signing off and clear with W9ZZO, Isle Royale, and W9ZZY, Devil's Island. S'long, fellas!"

Jim broke fast. "S'long, Katch. Say, will you be on in the morning? How about a sked?"

"Sure, I'll see you about 8:30, Jim. See you tomorrow."

Jim took it again. "Say, Jerry, this sounds like a pretty stiff blow. How about it? You think they should leave Duluth? Over."

"No, I sure don't. But all I can do is give them the weather reports. That skipper on the *Norcliff* is a salt water sailor and he doesn't take weather as an excuse to stay in port. He's taking an unnecessary chance, if you ask me. Over."

"You're not just whistling *Dixie!* How long will you be around?"

"I'm on watch till midnight."

"I think I'll hit the sack and get up early. If you're about then, give me a call. I'll be back on around seven."

"Okay, Jim. Everything will be all right but I'll give you a buzz at seven. Sleep tight, kid. W9ZZY off and clear with W9ZZO and leaving the air."

"W9ZZO clear." Jim secured the station and threw the antenna switch to the ground side. This was an automatic precaution, actually necessary only during the electrical storm season but a habit the rest of the time.

Everyone was in bed asleep when Jim returned to the

cabin. Setting the alarm for six, he, too, was soon fast asleep.

Mr. St. Cyr was up when the alarm rang and he stuck his head inside the door as Jim was turning it off.

"Bad weather, Jim. You got a sked?"

Jim nodded. "Yeah. Did you hear how Tim and Red made out?"

"Yes. They made it okay, but the end of the trip was pretty bad. There's a 50 mile nor-easter out there right now."

Jim dressed fast. He hurried to the kitchen where his father was dishing out two huge bowlfuls of oatmeal.

"Here," he said, "this'll stick to your ribs. The barometer has dropped. I'll have plenty of paper work to keep me tied up today." He filled two cups with strong, black coffee.

"I've got a couple of skeds this morning, then I'll be in." Jim gobbled down his oatmeal and pulled on his heavy jacket. He didn't want to bother with a fire this morning, at least not until he'd kept his schedules.

"Be back in a little while, Dad," he said as he slammed the door behind him.

The wind tore at him as he raced up the path to the shack. The room was still a little warm. He turned on the receiver first, then the transmitter. Signals blared at him from the loudspeaker. He looked at his watch, ten minutes until sked time, he thought.

"W9ZZY, this is W9ZZO. You around yet, Jerry?"

"W9ZZO, this is W9ZZY. Boy, am I glad you got on early. Katchy's ship is having a rough time of it. Somebody slipped up and the hatches weren't battened down tight enough. They've been taking water for the past hour. I'm not copying him too well . . . in fact, I've lost him completely on 51. Over."

Jim's face went white. "Where are they? Anyone on the way to help? Over."

"Yeah." Jerry was talking but another signal came on and covered him completely. Jim tuned frantically for an instant then—

"W9ZZO, W9ZZO, W8XI calling you. Do you copy?" When his signal cut off, Jim could hear Jerry still talking. No time to listen now. He threw on the transmitter.

"W9ZZO here. Roger! Loud and clear, Katch. Over!"

"Thank God! Jerry isn't getting me too good. The commercial rig quit. Tell him we're about twenty-five miles off Rock of Ages, on the downbound course. Find out if there's a ship near enough to help us. We're taking water fast. Pumps can't keep up. Hatches filling! Over."

"Roger! Roger. Stand by! W9ZZY, do you copy?"

Jim's lips were white as he spoke crisply into the microphone.

"W9ZZY here. Go ahead. I copy."

"*Norcliff* about twenty-five miles off Rock of Ages. Taking water fast. Needs help. Pumps can't keep up. Commercial gear dead. Needs help, I repeat, needs help fast! Over."

"Roger. Stand by to relay." Jerry left the transmitter on and Jim could copy him, even through the noise, as he talked on the commercial frequency 51.

"Emergency! Emergency! Mayday! *Norcliff* downbound twenty-five miles off Rock of Ages. Taking water

fast. Who is near enough to reach *Norcliff?* I repeat—
Mayday! Mayday! *Norcliff* in trouble. Over!"

Then Jim could hear another signal coming through
. . . but not loud enough to copy. Maybe his dad was
copying on 51, the clear channel frequency that the ships
and Coast Guard operated on. He hoped so. But he
couldn't leave long enough to find out—at least not yet.

Jerry was transmitting again. "Roger! Roger! Stand
by." Then his voice came through loud again as he spoke
to Jim.

"Do you copy, Jim?"

"I copy. Go ahead!"

"Tell Katch the S. S. *Rykes* is upbound and will be there
in about twenty minutes. They're going full speed ahead.
Over."

"Stand by." Jim's voice was tense, high pitched. He
was scared for his friend.

"Katchy! Katchy! Do you copy?"

"Roger, Jim." That was all.

"Katchy—the *Rykes* is upbound. Will be with you in
twenty minutes. Can you keep afloat that long?" Jim was
holding back the sobs now. This was his friend, his dear
friend Katchy, out there on Superior in a sinking ship.

"We'll try, Jim. We'll try. But she's going down fast.
Center deck awash—an'— S'long, kid! See you later.
W8XI/—" Then his signal cut off.

"Katchy! Katchy!"

"Jim! Jim!" Jerry's voice broke across the frequency.
"What's the matter?"

Jim couldn't speak, the knot in his throat was too big.
He left the carrier on. Finally he managed to say,

"Katchy's signals are gone. That tub is sinking—it's sinking, Jerry!"

"Hey, kid, they'll be okay. The *Rykes* just sighted them and they'll be alongside in ten minutes. Keep your chin up. Everything will be all right." Jerry was obviously trying to persuade himself as well as Jim. "Say, pal, can you stand by just in case we can't get through on 51? Just in case he comes back on?" Jerry's voice broke now.

"Yes, I'll stay here. Call me if you need me. W9ZZO, Isle Royale, standing by."

"Okay. I'll call you as soon as I know anything. W9ZZY clear."

Then the frequency went dead. Jim put his head on his arms and struggled again to control his fears for his friend Katchy. He must stay here; he might be needed. He wondered if his father had copied any of it. The ship was going down . . . He might never talk to Katchy again.

A few minutes later, Jim heard someone calling from the cabin. He pushed away from the desk, cold, numb and with an empty feeling inside. He opened the door. It was Jack calling him.

"Dad wants to know if you talked to Jerry. Some boat's sinking!" His voice was almost a scream.

"Yes," Jim called back. "Tell him I have to stand by in case I can do something more."

Jack turned and ran inside. A moment later he came back out.

"Okay," he called. "He says okay."

Jim walked back to his desk and sat before it, not hearing any of the noise coming in through the loudspeaker, only aware of the silence where Katchy's voice had been. ... He had tried to help, but it had not been good enough.

It was two hours later when Mr. St. Cyr sent Jack out to get Jim.

"Dad said to come in. He's talking to Devil's Island."

"I can't," Jim answered. "I promised—"

"But he says you're to come in. Jerry wants to talk to you on the clear channel frequency. Hurry up!" Jack ran back down the path and Jim pushed away from the desk again. He stumbled a little, cramped from sitting tense, waiting, listening, waiting for a call that never came.

He pulled the door shut. The wind blew his jacket open. The air was cold, penetrating. The water must be ice cold, too, he thought. The waves pounded against the rocks, against the beach, breaking fast and high in their struggle to outrace each other. Jim shivered.

Mr. St. Cyr was seated before the transmitter, earphones on. When he saw Jim, he pulled the phones off and turned on the speaker.

"Jerry wants to talk to you, Jim." He spoke loudly, above the noise coming in. Then, turning on the transmitter, he spoke briefly into the microphone.

"Here he is, Jerry. Over."

Jerry's voice came through. "Hi, kid." It filled the room grave, yet somehow tender.

The Ranger left his chair and pushed Jim into it. He nudged his son. "Talk, Jim. It's Jerry!" he urged gently. ... "Jim—"

The boy looked at the microphone as if it were a horrible monster. He hated it. He never wanted to see or use a microphone again.

"Talk to Jerry, Son. You won't be sorry." Mr. St. Cyr pressed Jim's shoulder with a kindly hand and Jack stood at his elbow, nudging him. "Please talk, Jim," the latter begged.

"Hi . . . Jerry."

"Say, kid." The voice still had a note of graveness in it, but it had something else, something almost reverent. "There's a friend on the frequency wants to talk to you. Take it away—WMZ, S. S. *Rykes.*"

Then a loud and strong carrier broke.

"How's tricks, Jim?" The expression on the boy's face changed from despair to disbelief.

He pushed the transmit switch with the speed of a darting bird.

"Katch? Is that really you, Katch?"

"Sure, kid." There was a moment's pause, "It's really me. Just wanted you to know we're okay—at least some of us. . . ."

Silence again as the carrier was stilled.

Jim couldn't talk. He didn't turn the transmit switch on. He just sat, eyes closed, saying a silent prayer of thanks.

Mr. St. Cyr reached over and pulled the microphone to him. "We'll see you later, Jerry, and you Katch—a little later."

"Roger," the operator aboard the *Rykes* answered.

Jim turned to his father. "They reached the *Norcliff* in time?"

"Well," the Ranger hesitated, "almost. They got more than half the crew off safely but lost seventeen men. The

Rykes will take the survivors back to Duluth. Katchy was one of the last to be picked up. He stuck to his post till the very last. You should be proud to have a friend like Katchy, Son." Mr. St. Cyr gently led the younger boys from the room.

Jim just sat there . . . for a long time.

16

vvvv • vvvv • vvvv • vvvv • vvvv • vvvv • vvvv

The days until Christmas flew swiftly past.

Jim had begun to wonder about his dad. The latter had been seeing Miss Gene several times a week and when he came back from each of his visits, he seemed quiet and thoughtful. Jim wanted to talk about his teacher, but every time he mentioned her, his father brushed him off, using work and reports as an excuse for not talking.

Whenever Jim hinted about radio school, it was still the same story. "Too young; no place for a seventeen-year-old; he wanted Jim to be a Ranger." The boy grew almost as quiet as his father.

The night before Christmas, the boys finished trimming the tree and hung their stockings on the fireplace in the living room. Then they sat around on the fur rug and Mr. St. Cyr told them stories.

"Now scoot to bed, small fry," he ordered finally.

A little later, he went into the younger boys' room to place a kiss on each smooth forehead after the earnest prayers were said.

In the meanwhile, Jim had slipped out to the shack to exchange a few more Christmas Eve messages with his friends. When he came in later, the cabin was quiet. The tree sparkled in the light of the fireplace and he said his prayers gazing wistfully at the star on the top.

In the morning, Chuck was the first to open his eyes. He bounced out of bed and dashed to the living room, then let out a shriek.

"He came! He came! Get up, everybody! Santa came while we were asleep!" He stared, round-eyed, at the bulging stockings hanging on the fireplace, then hopped around wildly.

At the first shout, the rest of the family hurriedly donned bathrobes and slippers and joined him, all calling "Merry Christmas" at the top of their voices. The noise was deafening, but Mr. St. Cyr, standing in the doorway, seemed to enjoy it thoroughly.

Seizing his hands, the boys danced him around in a circle until they were all breathless.

"For the love of Mike, let me sit! I'll be a wreck before I'm even dressed, if you aren't careful!" The Ranger flopped on the nearest chair to catch his breath.

"Look at the pile of packages under the tree!" Jack fell to his knees before them. "I'll call out the names and Chuck can deliver the presents."

Jack read aloud the messages on the handmade cards tied to each package, carefully and with an exaggerated flourish.

"To Dad, love and a Merry Christmas—from Chuck!" "To Jim, from Dad," and so on, to the last gift. Jim listened intently to everyone.

Then Mr. St. Cyr left the group around the tree and went out to the kitchen to start breakfast; Jim followed him.

"I'll help, Dad," he offered quietly.

Roger looked at his son out of the corner of his eye. "You don't sound much like Christmas, Jim. What's the matter?"

But Jim avoided Roger's glance. "Nothing," he answered shortly. Obviously his dad didn't want to talk radio today, or any day for that matter, and Jim wondered why he should be so stubborn about it.

Jim made an effort to enter into everything with the true Christmas spirit after that—but underneath it all was a feeling of disappointment that he had not received the one gift he most wanted—permission from his dad to take that radio course.

There were no vacations on Isle Royale except the long summer vacation. The teacher couldn't get away from the island in the winter, so school was held from late in the fall until the last of April.

The winter days passed quickly for everyone but Jim. He walked his trap lines every second day and his collection of pelts increased gradually. He hadn't once mentioned radio school to his father and he didn't realize that the Ranger was worried about his son's unaccustomed silence. Usually Jim talked over his problems with his dad, but since Christmas he had never asked his advice on anything. Instead, he spent more and more of his spare time in the radio shack and less time with the younger boys and his father.

One evening in April, Jim had retired to the radio shack early. He had several schedules to keep. One was with his friend in Houghton, at nine o'clock. Nothing new had developed at the college, so they settled down to a "rag-chew."

"Ever hear any more from that fellow up in Canada, Jim?"

"Sure. I have a checker game with him about once a week. Otherwise, whenever he's on and I hear him, I call him. He's a great guy. Did you ever talk to him?"

"Nope. I've heard you two gabbing away and I've eavesdropped on you a couple times, but I never have talked to him. He seems to be a swell fella. I heard you talking to him the day he got back from some place—when he told you that somebody up there wasn't the guy you were looking for."

"You did? We were talking about Duke. You remember the guy that ran away and left that boy here on the island?"

"Oh, I see. Say, whatever happened to the boy? Is he still staying at your place?"

"Yup! He's a nice kid, too," Jim approved

"What did you tell me his name was?"

"Peter Carey." Jim spoke casually into the mike.

"Hey—wait a minute!" Jim could hear the furious rattling of paper over the air, then, "Did you say Peter Carey?"

"Sure, why? And don't rattle that paper so much. It sounds like a forest fire. Wow! What a noise."

"Noise, nothing—listen to this." He quoted, "Anyone

knowing the whereabouts of a boy, aged ten, name Peter
Carey or Peter Everette, last heard of living with E. M.
Carey, Evansburg, Ohio, get in touch with the following
immediately. Drew and Field, Attorneys, 530 N. Duncan
Street, Cincinnati, Ohio." He drew in an audible gulp
of air. "What do you think of that? Could it be *your*
Peter?"

"Great guns! Read that slowly again, please. I want to
copy it. Go ahead. W9ZZO over to W9XXM." Jim was
so excited he almost forgot to sign his station call on the
fifteen-minute period lapse.

"This ad's been in about every paper around here for a
long time. Saw it in some big Sunday edition, too. Here
it is again." He repeated the entire ad, then signed.

"Golly Moses! I can't talk any more now. I think this
is it! See you tomorrow, same time, same frequency.
G'night!"

In his excitement, Jim even forgot to thank his friend.

Snatching up the written message, he turned off the
light in the shack and dashed up the path to the cabin,
yelling.

"Dad! Dad! Where are you anyway? Come here
quick!"

"Well," Mr. St. Cyr stood in the doorway of the living
room. "What seems to be ailing you? Calm down! You'll
wake the boys."

Clutching his father's arm, Jim turned him around and
pushed him into a chair. "Here! Read this!"

As Mr. St. Cyr read the message, his expressive face
showed surprise, then hopefulness. Perhaps they'd find
out something definite about Peter if this lead were genu-
ine. But it must be. No law firm would advertise for

anyone unless for some valid reason. Duke must have re-gained his senses and started a search for the boy.

"Where did you get this?" he asked finally, rousing him-self out of his absorption.

"It's from a Houghton paper. The fellow I talk to every night asked me what Peter's name was and then read this to me. He said it had been running for a long time."

Roger considered this carefully, then said, "It's too late to do anything about it tonight. Don't say anything to the boys until we find out more about the notice. I'll send the lawyers a message tomorrow, when I talk to Hough-ton. Go to bed now and get some sleep. School tomorrow —you know!"

"Okay, Dad." He was sorry his father wouldn't talk more about his discovery with him. For a moment his dad had seemed very close again, but evidently he wanted to be alone or he wouldn't chase a guy to bed so soon. Heck! At the door, Jim turned, "I almost forgot to tell you, these last two days of mild weather started the sap in the sugar bush."

"Isn't it a little early?"

"I thought so, too, but I tapped a tree last week and today there was sap in the pail."

"I'll take a run over to the pit and put out some buckets tomorrow. It shouldn't take me very long, with Star."

"How many buckets will you set out, Dad? Golly, we hardly had enough—"

"I can set out a few more this year. I think it was twenty last year, at three pounds per tree. I'll set out forty maybe this time. That ought to be plenty."

"It should, but you know how this bunch likes pan-cakes!"

"Well, we'll make forty do the trick. We can always set out a second run of buckets." Mr. St. Cyr bent over the slip of paper in his hand. "Run along now!" Evidently, his mind had already discarded the sugar bush for his new problem.

Jim turned away. His feet dragged and he kicked dejectedly at one of the throw rugs as he went to his bedroom. He wondered what this lead would amount to. Evidently it was important to the law firm to locate this missing Peter Carey or else why would they advertise in so many newspapers and for so long a time? Well, no use thinking any more about it tonight. His father didn't seem to want to discuss it with him. His mind went around in a circle. Slipping quietly into bed, he punched his pillow angrily. He wished he'd never heard of radio. After all, what good did it do him to know anything about it? Even a discovery like this didn't soften his dad so that he could talk to him reasonably.

At the breakfast table the next morning, Jim told the boys that the Ranger was going to set out the sap buckets.

"Jiminy! Are you, Dad?" Jack's freshly scrubbed face beamed with delight. He waved a crisp slice of bacon at Peter. "You'll like the sugar party—*mmm!*" He licked his lips in anticipation. "Maple sugar candy!"

"What do you have to do to get sugar?"

Jack's mouth was full so Jim answered Peter.

"First, you have to bore a hole with a three-eights-inch bit and auger. You have to be sure you get the sunny side of the tree, either south or east!" he explained. "The hole has to be bored on an upward slant, so that the sap will run out, and it should be about an inch and a half deep."

As he paused for breath, Peter urged, "Then what?"

"Then all you do is drive in a wood or metal spout and hang the bucket on the spout. Of course, you have to have a cover over the bucket so dirt doesn't drop in."

"And then is it maple syrup?"

"Course not," Chuck broke in between mouthfuls of toast and bacon, "you have to cook it."

Everyone laughed at this interruption. Chuck never had much time to talk when there was food in front of him.

"You see, Peter," Mr. St. Cyr explained, "we have to empty the buckets about noon. The greatest flow of sap is during the early morning. You boil down the sap until over half of the water has evaporated. There are thermometers to tell when you've boiled it enough, but we use the old Indian method. We pour a little out on the snow. If it gets waxy, then it's done."

Jack added his two cents worth. "That makes sugar. You don't boil it so long when you want to make syrup. We always have to make some of both. Golly, is it ever good—eating it off the snow!"

"You fellows will get out of school in time to help me boil it down tomorrow, so hurry home. I'll have the sugar stove already stoked."

Before Jim left for school with the younger boys, his father called him into the living room and handed him a sheet of paper. On it was a radio message for headquarters. "Have a Peter Carey, abandoned orphan, living with us. Signed Roger St. Cyr, Forest Ranger, Isle Royale, Michigan."

Jim nodded and said briefly, "Sounds okay to me." Then he hurried out to join the waiting boys on the porch.

Jim was the first to arrive home from school that afternoon. He'd not been able to apply himself to his lessons and finally Miss Gene gave up in despair. When school was dismissed; he grabbed his things and dashed up the trail. He wondered if his father had received an answer to the message about Peter. His even disposition wouldn't let him harbor a grudge for long and the radio school was sidetracked for the moment. He was anxious to discuss the lawyers' notice with his father.

When he entered the cabin, the Ranger exclaimed, "You're home early. You must have hurried."

"What did you find out?" Jim replied with a question.

"Nothing yet. I won't know until my next schedule. I only hope that we did the right thing in notifying those lawyers." He held a finger to his lips. "*Shh*—quiet, not a word to the boys! Here they come."

"Hi, Dad!" Jack's cap sailed across the room and almost found the hook it was aimed at. "What's cookin'?"

"Nothing, yet. I haven't been home long. I think I'll let you worry about supper. I've some work to finish." He motioned to Jim. "While the boys rustle up something to eat, you and I can do a little figuring in the radio room."

Jack regarded Jim and his father with a suspicious glint in his hazel eyes and Jim knew that his brother was sure something was going on. He couldn't quite get the drift, but he could smell excitement a mile away. This huddle in the radio room was out of the ordinary!

A few minutes later, Jim and his father emerged from their conference with cautious grins on their faces.

"If you don't look like a couple of birds that ate the cats, I'm crazy!" Jack cracked. "What's been going on?"

"Can't tell you anything now. Maybe later. Be patient and you'll know all about it then." Mr. St. Cyr drew his chair out from the table and sat down. "Something smells good. I believe I've worked up an appetite. By the way, if we have an early sun, we'll have some syrup to boil to-morrow."

"Yup, you told us that before." Jack wasn't to be side-tracked.

Chatter bounced back and forth from one to the other across the table. Spring fever had settled on the little group in earnest. Even Chuck broke in on his eating to plan aloud his spring colony cleaning. He was going to paint all his squirrel houses—if his father would donate the paint.

"You can't paint until the snow leaves," the Ranger reminded him. "We may have plenty of snow yet. You never know up here!"

"I can be ready though, can't I?" Chuck pouted.

Jim saved the day with his suggestion. "Of course you can. Why not take one house down at a time and bring it inside and paint it? Then they'll be set for the summer and you can put them all out together. The squirrels don't sleep in them, anyway!"

"Good idea," Chuck mumbled from his full mouth.

Mr. St. Cyr glanced at his watch as he finished his second cup of coffee. "Two minutes to six. Come on, Jim."

As the two hurried into the radio room again and closed the door, Jim heard Jack grumble, "This suspense is wearing me down. I wonder what they're up to. I never saw them act so funny before."

Peter spoke up quickly. "Don't bother about it. If you were supposed to know, they'd tell you. Come on. Let's get these dishes done."

At the radio, Mr. St. Cyr had turned off the loudspeaker and plugged in two sets of earphones. Handing one pair to Jim, he quickly slipped the other pair on his ears.

"Calling Houghton. Isle Royale calling and standing by."

"Houghton to Isle Royale. Right on the nose, Rog ol' man! Your message came through about four-thirty this afternoon. Got your pencil and paper ready?"

"Sure have," the Ranger answered briefly. "Shoot!"

"To Roger Blake, care Isle Royale Ranger Station, Isle Royale, Michigan. My client will arrive by plane April fifteenth, from Seattle, Washington. Peter Carey possibly Peter Everette. Have proof of identity ready. Signed Drew and Field. Guess that's all, Roger."

"That's enough! Thanks a lot for your trouble. Here's my report." The Ranger was busy for the next few minutes, sending his daily duties to headquarters.

"Golly, Dad!" Jim burst out the minute his father had finished. "What do you make of it?"

"I don't know, unless it might be some distant relatives looking for the boy. Peter has never mentioned anyone else, has he?"

"I don't know, not to me, anyway. He was an orphan and had no one until the Careys took him!" Jim answered. "Maybe they're giving him the Careys' farm. He was their adopted son, you know!"

"Well, it looks like we'll have to wait till April fifteenth to find out what this is all about. Those lawyers certainly didn't waste any words telling us whom to expect. Their client—humph!" Mr. St. Cyr puffed furiously on his newly lighted pipe. The smoke whirled in great gusts around his head.

Jim slid down into the deep easy chair and threw one leg over the arm, a favorite position of his. He seemed about to speak.

For one brief moment, he forgot the message in his hand.

"If you're thinking what I think you are," he observed dryly, "the answer is still no!"

Without a word, Jim rose slowly and walked from the room. At that instant he felt that his father could *never* understand him. He had been thinking only of Peter and his future.

17

vvvv • vvvv • vvvv • vvvv • vvvv • vvvv • vvvv

It was hard to concentrate on lessons to-day. The sun came through the windows and made dancing patches of light.

Jim had told Miss Gene of the sugar party, so she knew the reason for the daydreaming. The Butlers and Johnsons, fisherfolk from Chippewa Harbor, had hung out their buckets yesterday, and Doris and Helen Butler and the Johnson children were squirming restlessly when the clock registered two-thirty.

Finally, Miss Gene gave up in despair. "You children might as well go home now. Your minds are certainly not on your lessons," she said hopelessly—but she smiled understandingly.

"I wish you were coming to our party, Miss Gene," Jim said as he pulled on his coat.

"I wish I were, too, Jim," she answered, "but the Johnsons have invited me to their party. I'm as anxious to get away from here as you are!" She was pulling on her boots and coat as she talked and Jim knew she was telling the truth.

The mad dash for home began, Jim in the lead. It lasted until the four boys were all puffing along, winded and red of face. Then they slowed down to a fast walk.

They could see the smoke of the fire in the clearing long before they topped the ridge. There was very little wind today, and the smoke curled lazily up over the tree tops and rose high into the blue-and-white sky.

At the edge of the clearing, the younger St. Cyrs and Peter let out a war whoop and raced down the trail to the cabin. Jim followed more slowly. When he came up to the others, Jack was saying, "Miss Gene let us out early. She's going to a sugar party at the Johnsons. Golly, isn't this a swell day?" He gave the fire a poke with a stick that had fallen to one side of the oven.

His father nodded in agreement and announced, "Well, we're all set. Jack, you and Peter can fetch the syrup pan from the storehouse, while Jim and I get the sap."

"Did we get a nice run, Dad?" Jim asked as he walked along beside his father.

"A dandy!" the Ranger answered. "It took me all day to get it back here. I put the keg on the sled and Star dragged it six trips. I left the buckets out. We may as well make what we can."

Jim and his father poured pailful after pailful of the thin liquid into the long, deep pan that rested in the sugar oven, while the youngsters hung eagerly around and got underfoot. The St. Cyrs had built the syrup oven three years before. Made of bricks and sealed with mortar, it looked like a long watering trough. In reality, it was seven feet long, three feet high and three feet wide. The heavy galvanized pan that held the watery syrup was six feet long and eighteen inches deep and served as the top or lid of the stove.

The aromatic smell of pinewood smoke and the sound of the sharp sparks that leaped from the tamarack, to crackle and fizzle and then fade inside their nest of brick seemed to make a deep impression on the youngsters.

Finally the sap bubbled—first hesitatingly, then with a persistent force that made the water evaporate into clouds of steam.

The boys, armed with long-handled spoons from the cabin, kept the steadily boiling syrup from plopping over the top.

About six o'clock Jim went to the cabin and, within a few minutes, reappeared with a heaped platter of sandwiches and a pitcher of hot chocolate.

Sugaring was a tiresome job and a long one, but the younger boys didn't appear to notice it until about eleven o'clock.

"Golly, Dad, when do you think this stuff will be done? I'm getting tired," Jack announced from his side of the oven.

"It shouldn't take much longer, Jack. Why don't you and Peter sit on the sled with Chuck and rest?" Mr. St. Cyr continued to stir slowly as he spoke. The syrup was getting heavy now. He spooned some out on a nearby drift of snow. "Here, try it and see how it tastes!"

Peter and Jack ran over to the drift and picked up the stiff strands that had hardened as the syrup hit the snow.

"Mmmmmm, is this good!" Peter seemed amazed at the change of the watery sap into chewy, delicious candy.

Chuck roused himself from his cozy seat on the sled

near the oven and ambled over for his share of the sticky candy.

"The only thing I don't like about making syrup—it takes too long! When do we eat?" He glowered sleepily at the group.

"It'll be a midnight snack for you tonight, I'm afraid." His father laughed. "You would stay up, you know. I'll bet school tomorrow will be a droopy affair!"

"We'll have lots of company, then. Miss Gene and the rest of the gang from Chippewa Harbor won't get any more sleep than we do," Jim observed.

"I think this'll be thick enough, and we aren't going to sugar off tonight. If the sap keeps on running as it has, we'll have about four nights at this job." Mr. St. Cyr sighed. He was getting weary, too.

"I'll get the jugs from the cabin, Dad." Jim put down his spoon and rubbed his tired muscles. He walked up the path to the house, to return shortly with a load of gallon jugs in which to seal the hot syrup.

"I'll certainly enjoy maple syrup more, now that I've stirred my arms off making it," Peter grunted from his seat on the sled.

Apparently his curiosity had been thoroughly satisfied for one day. He didn't offer to help pour the thick syrup into the jars.

While Jim and the boys carried the full jugs into the storehouse, Mr. St. Cyr spread the fire in the oven so that it would die out, then followed the others to the cabin. While the boys were donning pajamas, he fixed sandwiches, poured hot chocolate and cut huge slices of cake.

It was a weary bunch that finally crawled under the inviting bed covers. Before Jim had finished banking the kitchen fire, the younger boys were fast asleep. He grinned to himself—and promptly followed their example.

School routine suffered from the sugar parties. Everyone, Miss Gene included, drooped. Jim was glad when, at noon the next day, she proclaimed a holiday.

"As long as we're all in this sugaring bee for the duration of the run, we may as well dismiss school," she announced. "You're excused until Thursday. The run should be over by then. Maybe we can act normal when we get our proper rest!"

Jim didn't join in the screams and shouting that shook the schoolroom. He was relieved, however, to know that now he'd have a little time for a few radio schedules.

The next two days were lively ones.

Jim and the boys helped Mr. St. Cyr bring in the kegs of sap from the sugar bush and the fire in the oven was started as soon as the huge vat was filled.

They finally worked it out into a system. While Jim and his father stirred the liquid, to keep it from boiling over or sticking to the bottom of the vat, Jack and Peter, with Chuck and Hill Billy trailing behind, would prepare plates of sandwiches and pans of hot chocolate and steaming coffee. Then, while Jim and his father rested and ate, Peter and Jack took their turn with the spoons.

The fourth day of the run started as usual. At six o'clock, the Ranger made a brief report to the mainland, then hurried back to the syrup oven.

A few minutes later, Jim stopped stirring long enough to turn his head and listen intently.

"Do you hear anything?" he asked his father.

"Sounds like a plane." Jack observed from his seat on the sled.

He and Peter and Chuck had been busy eating so that they could stir while Jim and Mr. St. Cyr ate.

"It does sound like a plane, but it's getting fainter. Can't be coming here," Mr. St. Cyr remarked and resumed the monotonous stirring.

"Funny time for a plane to be coming to the island," Jim muttered, more to himself than to anyone else. "It's almost dark."

"I'll stir for a while now. I'm through eating." Jack took the long spoon from Jim's hand.

"Golly, does my arm ache!" Jim rubbed his forearm vigorously and made a face. "Wow! How many more gallons are we going to make?" He groaned wearily as he sat on the sled with his father.

"We've got over twenty gallons now. I think tonight will finish off the syrup for this year. No sense in getting more than we can use."

Jim suggested, "How about some music, Peter?"

Peter's face lit up in a happy smile. "Sure! I'll go get my mouth-organ!"

Jim nodded and took a huge bite from a fresh sandwich. Only the scrape, scrape of the wooden spoons on the bottom of the long pan broke the stillness.

When they had started the sugaring earlier that day, the sun was high and warm in the sky. Now, the stars twinkled brightly and the moon made silvery patterns on the drifts of white snow.

When all the songs that they knew had been sung, Peter played some of the numbers that Miss Gene had helped him learn. Then he drifted into the haunting, un-

finished lullaby that seemed to float up from the deepest
pocket of his heart. He played it over and over again. It
lulled them all into a dreamy silence.

The dull sound of the wooden spoons hitting on the
syrup pan was like an obligato to Peter's rhythmic tune.
The sweet, sugary odor, mixed with pine, rose like in-
cense into the nostrils of the little group.

Suddenly a new note added itself to the sound of the
mouth-organ, the sound of a woman's voice humming the
melody. It seemed to blend with the soft music and
the little audience listened intently, not moving, scarcely
breathing lest this new tone be silenced.

Even when Peter held his mouth-organ rigidly in his
hand, the sound kept on. No one moved. The stillness in
the clearing was almost ghostly as the lullaby continued
to come out of the darkness.

Jim's eyes sought Peter and an eerie feeling gripped
him as he saw the boy held spellbound. Where was this
music coming from, music that Peter wasn't making? Obviously, it was the rest of the lullaby flowing out of the
night—the rest of the lullaby Peter couldn't ever seem to
remember! Or was he only imagining this? No, it couldn't
be! He peered quickly into the faces around him. On
each was written an expression of wonder and breathless
inner excitement. Then the melody stopped.

The tense group around the glowing oven stared at
each other with the same question on the tips of their
tongues. Did they imagine the song, or were they all
dreaming?

A quick peal of laughter brought them about, startled,
to face a small knot of people emerging from the darkness
at the edge of the cabin.

"Hi there, St. Cyr! We got through earlier than usual today. Have a little surprise for you." The booming voice of the tall fisherman from Chippewa Harbor rocketed toward them. The swaying beams from their flash lights defined three pairs of feet, one a woman's, drawing nearer to the fire.

Mr. St. Cyr found his voice and greeted the newcomers with quick relief.

"Where the dickens did you drop from, Johnson? We didn't hear you coming!"

"We came in the fishing boat—quicker at night, you know," Mr. Johnson stated, as he entered the pale glowing ring cast by the hot sugar oven. "I've got some company here for you."

At his side stood a young woman dressed in dark blue slacks and a tan leather flying jacket. Her dark hair was held back by a pale band of ribbon. Her dark eyes flashed in the firelight.

"I do hope you'll forgive us for arriving like this," she said as she walked toward the Ranger with outstretched hand. "My husband and I got lost coming across the Lake and landed at the wrong place."

"But I don't understand," Mr. St. Cyr smiled at the earnest face looking up at him in the flickering light. "There must be some mistake."

"I don't believe so. You see—we're from Drew and Field."

Roger started at hearing this firm name and then looked quickly at Jim. "Oh, I understand now, but we weren't expecting you for two days." He paused, "The lawyers radioed me—"

She interrupted him. "Yes, I know we're a few days

ahead of schedule, but when I had word from my lawyers I couldn't wait a minute longer. We flew to Ohio from Washington. My name is Corby, Ellen Corby and this is my husband—Dwight!"

The two men shook hands. Obviously, Roger liked the cleancut looks of this very tall fellow. Jim judged him to be about thirty-five years old. He was athletic in build, with strong, rugged features, topped by a sandy-blond thatch of closely cropped hair.

"I'm glad to know you, Mr. St. Cyr," Dwight Corby said in a rich bass voice. "I hope this journey will prove a success, I've been athletic coach at Morton College, in Washington. I accepted a better position at the College of Mines in Houghton a few weeks ago and I'm due on the job there in a few days."

The younger boys had stood silent through all this. Jim and Jack automatically continued to stir the syrup, while Peter sat on the sled with Chuck, his mouth-organ clutched tightly in his hand.

"We are finishing up this batch of syrup, then we can go to the cabin and talk." Mr. St. Cyr glanced over at Peter, then spoke in a low voice to Mr. Corby. "I haven't told him anything yet. I thought it best not to give the boy any false hopes until we had proof."

"I think you're right." Mr. Corby agreed in an undertone, then continued more loudly, "This looks like fun. Mind if I stir a little?"

"Not at all." Roger handed him a spoon, "This is a critical point in making the syrup, so I don't dare leave it until it's done."

Mrs. Corby sat down between Peter and Chuck on the sled. "Let's sing some more while they're busy," she suggested. "The music sounded so beautiful, drifting across the water as we came into the dock, that I couldn't resist singing along with you." She put an arm lightly around each of the boys. "Won't you play that last song again? I love it!"

"I love it, too." Peter spoke quietly to this nice person who sat beside him. "I never heard the ending, until you finished it." He looked at her gravely. "Will you sing it again so that I can learn it?"

"Of course I will!"

The strange, haunting melody again floated across the clearing, only this time, instead of stopping after the first few bars and repeating them hesitantly, Peter played straight through to the end—a little haltingly perhaps, but with Mrs. Corby singing the melody, it seemed that he knew each new measure.

While the men stirred the syrup, they talked of everything but the subject that was naturally uppermost in their minds. Jim wanted to blurt out a dozen questions, but he didn't dare.

At last the syrup was done. Part of it was poured into jugs and the rest was boiled down more until it made a waxy candy on the snow. The workers drained the huge pan of thick liquid into long flat trays and carried them to the storehouse to cool. This would crystallize and turn into maple sugar. The entire party was munching huge chunks of maple candy as they walked to the cabin.

At the porch, Mr. Johnson said, "I've got to get back home. Can you put these people up, Roger?"

"Certainly, and thanks a lot for bringing them over."

"Better get ready for bed, boys," Mr. St. Cyr said as they entered the cabin. Then he turned to his guests.

"Will you come in here where we can talk?" He led the way into the living room. Jim shooed the younger boys into the bathroom to wash, then followed his father and their guests into the living room. He didn't intend to miss a thing, if he could help it!

"Mr. St. Cyr, you don't know what this means to me. It's almost too good to be true!" Mrs. Corby touched her eyes with her handkerchief.

"How did you ever come to advertise for this child? He was put in the orphanage when he was two or three, wasn't he?" Mr. St. Cyr asked and Jim waited tensely for the answer.

"We never would have known anything about him if I hadn't had to send back for family information and a birth certificate for my new civil service job." Mrs. Corby was struggling to hold back her tears. "The clerk said that, after Mother and Dad died, my baby brother was sent to an orphanage. You see, I'd been living for years with my grandparents in Seattle. They had quarreled bitterly with my parents about something or other when I was a small girl, so I lost touch with my family and didn't even know I had a brother. In fact, because my grandparents never spoke about my mother and father, I took it for granted that they had already died." She drew a deep breath and her voice was steadier when she began again.

"When Dwight and I knew for sure that I had a brother somewhere, we engaged lawyers to locate him. Drew and Field finally discovered that the Careys had adopted him and he grew up as their son. Then they died and the boy disappeared with the hired man who worked on the farm for the Careys."

Mr. St. Cyr broke in here. "When we found Peter, he'd

been abandoned by a man called Duke, who had worked
for a family named Carey. Peter is sure that Duke hurt
his head when he fell into a mine pit near their camp. We
haven't been able to find a trace of him since he disappeared."

"That is what I've been waiting to hear. It all fits together now."

"Then you are certain that this boy is your brother?"

"If I was uncertain before, tonight cleared my mind of
all doubt. When I heard the lullaby coming across the
water to me, I knew that I had found my brother at last."
Her eyes were bright with unshed tears. "It seemed like
a miracle. You see, Mother came from Scotland. She used
to sing this old Scottish lullaby to me when I was a very
little girl, before my grandparents took me out West.
Mother was in a T.B. sanatorium when they took me.
Always expecting, of course, to bring us together when
she got well. So you see, Peter must have heard it from
our mother, too."

"He was very young when she died," Mr. St. Cyr reminded her.

"Yes, but even a very young child has a memory. He
may not remember Mother, but the melody she sang night
after night, when she rocked him to sleep, must have
made an indelible impression on his baby mind. I am sure
of it. I've never heard anyone but our mother sing that
song!"

"I'm glad for Peter that you have found each other. He
has made a place for himself in our family circle that we
shall find very empty when he leaves us." The Ranger
cleared his throat sharply.

The lump in Jim's throat wouldn't budge!

Mrs. Corby cried out passionately, "But think what it will mean to him to know that he has found one of his own family—and Dwight and I will love him and take good care of him!"

Mr. Corby leaned forward and put his arm about his wife's shoulders.

"I think we can call him in now." Mr. St. Cyr walked slowly to the door of the younger boys' bedroom. "Peter, come here please. I've some very good news for you."

Peter stood in the open doorway, holding tightly to the Ranger's hand.

The latter squeezed the small hand in his. "You're a very lucky little boy, Peter. This lady is your sister and this is her husband. You are going to live with them in Houghton!"

Peter's eyes and mouth flew open. He stood as still as a small statue while two big tears rolled down his cheeks and fell unheeded. Then, with a low sob, he threw himself into Mrs. Corby's arms.

"Is it true? Is it true?" he kept saying over and over and the lump in Jim's throat threatened to choke him now.

"Yes, dear, it's true, every word of it." Mrs. Corby held Peter close, as if she meant never to let him go again.

The clock on the mantelpiece pointed to one o'clock before all questions had been asked and answered. Then they trooped out to the kitchen for a snack and sat around the table, laughing and talking. It was indeed the time for celebration. Jack and Chuck were wakened by the commotion and hurried to join in the fun. Hasty explanations followed.

Chuck stopped eating long enough to ask, "Golly, you

won't be able to go on any more picnics with us, will you, Peter?"

Mrs. Corby cut short the sighs that followed the half-question, half-statement. "But we want you all to come to Houghton to visit Peter this summer. There are ever so many exciting things to see and places to go." She studied Peter's serious face. "Of course we can fly over this summer and visit here, too. So don't worry, there'll be plenty of picnics."

At that, smiles bloomed all around the table again.

"You all will come over this summer to see us, won't you?" Mrs. Corby insisted as she leaned over to look straight at the Ranger.

"We'll have to wait until I can get a vacation," he started to reply, grinning at the excited, shining faces around the table. But the question he saw in Jim's eyes made him hesitate and leave the rest unsaid.

18

vvvv • vvvv • vvvv • vvvv • vvvv • vvvv • vvvv

It was a jolly group that climbed the schoolhouse steps the next morning.

Mr. and Mrs. Corby had accompanied the boys so that they could learn about Peter's grades and which class he should be ready to enter in a Houghton school next fall. The Corbys had already met Miss Gene the day before, when they landed at Chippewa Harbor.

The schoolteacher said, as she held Mrs. Corby's hand in a warm clasp, "I've been anxious to hear whether Peter was really your brother or not. It's a wonderful thing for him." She added hastily, "Not that he hasn't been happy with the St. Cyrs, but for him to find a sister is about perfect." She took Jim's hand with her free hand and shook it. "And you can thank Jim for that, Mrs. Corby—Jim and his wonderful ability as an amateur radio operator."

The boy could feel the flush slowly mounting to his ears. She was on his side, after all. He returned the handshake.

"I don't understand." Dwight frowned a bit. "In what way do you mean, Miss Gene?"

"If Jim hadn't been on the air and good friends with these other ham radio fellows on the mainland, you probably would never have found Peter!" She went all out for Jim now and gave them information about his tireless quest over the air for information that might help clear up the mystery about Peter, that had not been mentioned before, not because it had been omitted intentionally but because it had been taken as a matter of course.

After these explanations, Mrs. Corby put both her hands on Jim's shoulders. She was much shorter than he and he looked down into her face as she talked.

"You've made everything so perfect for us, Jim!" she said softly. "Dwight and I want to give Peter the love and care and education that rightly belong to him. I decided not to work if we were lucky enough to find Peter."

Dwight Corby nodded emphatically. "You all have already done more than most people would do and we can never repay you. I wish we could spend more time on the island, but we can only stay one more day. I have to report in Houghton day after tomorrow."

Finally good-bys were said and then the Corby's left for Chippewa Harbor, to get their plane. Peter and the St. Cyrs were to see them again at noon.

An hour later, the children in school heard the plane circle overhead, then fly off in the direction of the St. Cyr cabin. When Jim and the boys raced home after school, they saw the plane riding at anchor near the end of the dock.

It was almost six o'clock when Jim pushed his chair

abruptly back from the table and excused himself to the laughing group who were finishing an early supper.

"I've got a schedule with Houghton. This is our checker night. I'll be in early." He turned to Dwight Corby with his charming grin. "Come out and see the shack, if you have a minute!"

"I'd like to. A friend of mine back in Washington is a ham. Ever talk to Washington?"

"Sure, lots of times!" Jim answered.

"Seattle?" Mr. Corby wondered.

"Yes. I don't remember their calls, but I've talked to several of the fellows out there."

"I'll be along in a few minutes," Mr. Corby promised, "just as soon as I have another cup of this good coffee."

As Jim slammed the kitchen door, Mrs. Corby exclaimed, "There goes a very alert young man, Mr. St. Cyr!"

"What makes you say that?" Jim's father was inclined to agree with her, but modestly challenged her remark.

"Any boy that can do the things he can do, must be exceptional."

"While you two are discussing Jim, I'll go out to the shack for a few minutes. I'd like to see his station." Mr. Corby strode after Jim.

Mrs. Corby insisted on helping with the dishes, and soon had the whole crowd busy wiping them, trying to keep up with her swift washing.

Hill Billy jumped up and down on Chuck's shoulder and scolded as the boy hustled back and forth, in and out of the pantry. Hill Billy was hungry and he knew that a box of nuts reposed on the top shelf. Openly resentful at being ignored, he finally leaped to the shelf and helped himself through a small hole Roger had cut in the side of the box.

Out in the shack, the young college coach slid quietly into a chair beside Jim and watched with interest the checker game that was in progress. Jim won the first game, then said seriously, "Sorry, old man, I've got company. I'll play a game with you tomorrow night, if you're going to be around. How about it?"

"Okay, Jim. See you tomorrow night, same time, same frequency. 73." And the voice from across the vast expanse of Lake Superior's deep, chill water was still after he signed with his call.

"Would you like to talk to anyone, Mr. Corby? If you would, I'll try to hook someone out in a western state!"

"Not tonight. I must only stay a few minutes. There are a few things we must straighten out before we leave tomorrow." He looked around the cluttered room. "Did you ever think of going on with radio, Jim? Seems to me that's your line!"

"It's my whole life, Mr. Corby." Jim's face was alight with earnestness. "I wanted to go to summer school in Houghton this coming summer, but Dad thinks I'm too young to leave home and be on my own and besides, he wants me to be a Ranger. I can't seem to convince him that I could take care of myself."

"It appears to me that you're pretty capable for a seventeen-year-old! Many boys leave home younger than that!"

"Maybe, but Dad doesn't think so. He has set his heart on my being a Forest Ranger. I'd hate to disappoint him. He's so swell and everything to us kids—."

"Perhaps he thinks you'll change your mind."

"Maybe." Jim signed his logbook, and shoved it aside.

Then he said wistfully, "Guess I'll have to give up my summer school idea for this year, anyhow."

Dwight Corby banged his closed fist on his knee. "I've got it! Why couldn't you stay with us in Houghton for the summer and go to radio school? We'd like to have you, and besides," he reasoned, "you'd be company for Peter!"

Jim leaped to his feet. "Golly! If I only could!"

"Well, why couldn't you? You certainly would be safe with us, and Mrs. Corby would love to have you."

"Do you really mean it? You're not saying it just to be nice to me?"

"Of course I mean it. Let's go ask your dad now, shall we?"

But Jim was already halfway up the path.

He burst through the cabin door and in one breath poured out Dwight Corby's suggestion and invitation.

"So you see, Dad, I'd be perfectly safe with Mr. and Mrs. Corby. May I go?" The resigned expression that had haunted his face for the past few months was gone and in its place was a look of hopeful longing. "I'd like to have a chance at least to try out radio."

Roger St. Cyr smiled at his guests. "I suppose so." His voice was sure now. All the reserve and tightness was gone. What Jim didn't know was that his father had gradually changed his mind and hadn't realized it himself until now. "It never hurts to try out a thing, to be perfectly sure. And if Jim stays with you, I'll know he's in good hands."

"We'd love to have him, Mr. St. Cyr. It'll be company for all of us," Mrs. Corby offered enthusiastically.

"And as you suggest, it will give him a good chance to

find out for sure whether or not he wants to go on with radio," added her husband.

"It's only for three months, Dad—" Jim's voice had a husky quality in it.

"Don't worry, Jim," his father began a bit awkwardly, as if he didn't know quite how to continue. "I hadn't any idea that it really meant so much to you. We can manage without him, can't we, fellas?" He directed this last question to Jack and Chuck, who were sprawled on the floor in front of the fireplace.

Jack gazed solemnly at his father. "Sure—at least I think so. And say, Dad, maybe I can help with the radio reports an' stuff—" He looked at Jim then. "And maybe I could use your binoculars?"

Jim smiled. The lump in his throat melted and his whole body seemed to relax as he answered. "You sure can." He grinned at Roger then, "I think he'd make a mighty swell Ranger, don't you?"

HELEN H. CLOUTIER

has been a class "A" radio operator since 1929. She used a small bit of her accumulated information about ham radio as authentic background for her first published book, *Isle Royale Calling*.

Born in Manistique, Michigan, Mrs. Cloutier studied journalism and creative writing at Northwestern University and library science at Marquette College. She received her B.A. from the University of Los Angeles. She has taught creative writing in the Michigan adult education system, taught radio for the U. S. Air Force during World War II, owned and operated her own beauty shop, worked on the staff of the *Escanaba Daily Press*, was continuity director-announcer for radio station WESK-NBC for three years. At present she is working as secretary and assistant to the consultant of the Upper Peninsula Branch of the Michigan State Library.

Mrs. Cloutier also is a freelance writer-photographer. Her work has appeared in many trade magazines and newspapers such as *American Forests, Varsity, Radio and Television News* and the *Milwaukee Journal*.

Her occupations have included owning and teaching in a dancing school, pianist in dance bands, playing pipe organ in a theater, raising and selling chinchillas. Her hobbies are ham radio, oil painting and growing flowers.

Her ham station equipment includes a Globe King 400 watt all band transmitter, an HT-9 transmitter, SX-25 and S-20R receivers, a Meissner Signal Shifter for VFO. She has mobile equipment in her car, an Elmac transmitter and Morrow Converter. She operates phone and cw on all bands. She became the *first* woman member of the Quarter Century Wireless Association in 1954.